Paige Newhart is a highly successful author, gaining fame for her romantic novels and known to her readers as the Queen of Romance. Paige has a luxurious penthouse, loads of money, designer clothes, and all the trappings of success, but she has never found a hero of her own.

At forty-eight, Paige decides to finally take the plunge to find true love and sets her sights on writing a new love storyline for herself. Despite her success at writing romance, she knows finding true love in real life is not easy, especially at her age.

Then she meets Booker Turner. Wildly attractive, he is her complete opposite but ticks all her boxes.

Can Paige find true love and trust, or will she settle for just writing about it?

Mountain Match
Copyright © 2024 Kathy Kalmar
ISBN: 978-1-4874-3521-9
Cover art by Martine Jardin

Published by eXtasy Books Inc

Look for us online at:
www.eXtasybooks.com

MOUNTAIN MATCH
MOUNTAIN 17

BY

KATHY KALMAR

DEDICATION

Dedication Larry: Yesterday, today, tomorrow, and Forever, world's best partner and beta reader.

In Memoriam

Linda and Ron Wilson.
Mom and Dad, who introduced me to the mountains and always encouraged this dream.

In Acknowledgement

Carolynn Gilbreath, words fail to convey the depths of my feelings for her friendship, the truest brand of perfect friend and her contributions to this work. Jay Austin, Editor in Chief for making my dream come true, Bri, for polishing my words, Debbie Nygaard, amazing editor and more, Martine Jardin, artist, The Greater Detroit Romance Writers, Doug Marple, webmaster, and you, my fans.

CHAPTER ONE: THOUGHTS FROM A FEVERED BRAIN

Paige Newhart had it all. That was what she told herself, anyway. True, she had the job of her dreams and lived in her dream house—a penthouse. Still had her fame with the big bank account to show for it. She even had the proverbial dog everyone talked about, thanks to her recently acquired stepbro, Tex, and his last visit. When she saw the monster pup, she told Tex, "It's on probation. This is not a forever home."

Her thoughts returned to her present plight. *Somewhere, somehow, something's missing in my life, and it makes my brain ache.*

A blinding pain ripped through Paige's head. She raised a shaking hand to her forehead and massaged it. *Oh God, am I having a stroke?* Nausea rolled through her, and she groped for the wastebasket in case she had to hurl.

Dizziness overwhelmed her, adding more misery on top of her throbbing headache. *Is this an aneurysm?* She eased herself from her ergonomic chair and slipped to lay on the gray-colored hardwood floor, mercifully missing her well-organized desk with its pens and pencils—well sharpened and arranged just so. The floorboards felt cool against her cheek.

Ice. Maybe ice will stop the pain. Paige didn't want to risk standing up to get some. She rolled onto her back, holding her head between her hands, trying to stop the pain or at least keep it at bay. It didn't work. *Calm down. Maybe it's not a stroke.*

She could hear her older sister's voice in her head, counseling her to breathe. *"Inhale."* She inhaled and felt like puking. *"Exhale."* She got dizzier.

Tiny — the pooch on probation — licked her hands, whining as if worried. Or more likely, wanting to go outside. Paige pushed the pup's head away, which didn't deter the imp. Tiny moved closer and licked her throbbing brow. When Paige turned her head to the side, Tiny began to bark, the sound feeling like shards of glass worming through her brain.

Paige wanted to shoot herself to end her suffering. Instead, she raised her index finger to her nose in the *quiet command* hand sign. "Quiet." Tiny didn't heed her and barked all the louder, bouncing back and forth in a near frenzy. "Tiny, stop. Settle. I'm okay."

Tiny produced another worried whine, then began drooling on her forehead, which pooled beneath her fingertips.

Paige groaned as she wiped the slime away. "Tiny, stop. I haven't passed out. I'm awake."

Through her pain, she heard pounding on the door and the dogwalker's voice calling out.

"Paige, you okay in there?"

She heard the lock turn, and then Alex was bent over her, soothing and petting the dog while firing off questions.

"Hey, you, okay? Did you fall? Have you forgotten to eat again? How long have you been working? Can you sit up?"

Paige noticed the security keycard she had given him lying on the floor. "Better pocket that before Tiny eats it."

Alex laughed. "Yeah. Good idea. That dog will eat anything."

"Tell me about it. He ate my Louis Vuitton pumps."

Alex shrieked. "Oh no, he did not." He paused and tilted his head, clearly considering the situation. "At least he has good taste."

"You mean expensive taste. Help me up, will ya?"

Alex pulled her up to a sitting position and gave her an odd look. "Talk to me. Say a complete sentence."

She frowned. "Why on earth would I do that?"

Alex scrunched his brow. "A question counts as a sentence, doesn't it?"

"Probably. What is this, some kind of test?"

Alex ignored her question and commanded, "Raise your arms above your head."

Paige lifted a brow instead. "Why?"

"Just do it."

She was tempted to roll her eyes but did as he asked.

Alex took her chin and tilted her head this way and that. "Hmm." His gaze roamed her face and then her body. He grinned. "Nothing's drooping." He paused when he got to her boobs. "Well, your face isn't, anyway."

"Very funny."

"You're not showing the typical signs of a stroke, so what gives?" He fished in his pocket, withdrew a small container, and shook out two pills. "Take these two aspirins. Just in case."

She gratefully took the pills with the water he handed her. "I'm fine. I have a monster migraine. I slid outta my chair, I didn't fall."

"You know that's not normal, right? You're killing yourself. And why? Yesterday, Elyse mentioned that you have no deadline to meet. No new books to write at the moment. No book signings or tours. Why do you push yourself so hard?"

Her cheeks heated. *He has me there.* "You don't stay on the best sellers list by lying around. I have work to do."

"Working yourself to death isn't going to cut it either. Even the airlines know to tell the passengers to put their masks on first so they don't pass out before they help their youngsters." He frowned. "Though judging from their recent performance, it doesn't appear like they know much about customer satisfaction." He shrugged. "But I digress. Writing from dawn to dusk day in and day out is not the way to keep your mojo flowing. You need some downtime. Have to recharge the battery. I prescribe a nice relaxing vacay."

"Thank you very much," Paige grumbled. "But I already have a mother, you know. And an older sister."

Alex shook his head. "Yeah."

She shot him a wry look. "You're my dogwalker."

"Nuh-uh. From now on, I'll be your assistant.

"Elyse is my assistant."

"She was your assistant — *was* being the operative verb. She left. Remember? Don't tell me you didn't notice?" He rocked, holding his arms as if cradling a baby. "You know . . . The baby bump? The maternity leave? Maybe you did have a stroke."

Paige groaned. "Of course, I remember."

Alex continued. "Now that we know for sure you haven't had a stroke, starting today, I'll handle your schedule, make you eat, sleep, dress. For heaven's sake, you make six figures, yet you dress like a bag lady! You need a keeper to make sure you do the things normal people do. When was the last time you poured yourself a glass of wine and took a good old-fashioned bubble bath? Or better yet, used your ultra-sonic shower stall with its piped-in music, aromatherapy, and chromotherapy system?"

Paige gaped at him. "How do *you* know about my shower?"

Alex pointed at her mutt. "Ahem, I groom Tiny. He wallows in every mud puddle he finds. I have to clean him up."

"You do? Using my shower?"

Alex shrugged. "Someone's gotta do it."

"Don't I have a dog groomer for that?"

"Yes, you do, but take it from me, you'd go broke fast if I took that lummox in every time he did his doggy best to roll around in horse manure in Central Park. Not to mention the bushes, leaves, you name it, and don't even get me started on thistles."

"Thistles?"

"He loves plowing through them in search of chipmunks."

Paige held a hand up to stop his flow of info. "Okay, okay. So, you wash him off in my state-of-the-art bathroom?"

Alex smiled. "Yup. He adores the summer rain and lavender spray. I prefer the summer sun, myself." He nodded. "Your puppy makes a mess, and I can't be a wet, hot mess after grooming him, ya know? I even keep an extra set of clothes here. You never notice, because your face is glued to your keyboard."

Paige waved that off. "My process is to write from six to six. I have to research, plot, consult my thesaurus, run through my emotion's encyclopedia, dust off *The Elements of Style*, browse my urban dictionary, check my goal, motivation, conflict, my outline . . ." Her writing style made her a proverbial plotter. Every scene was researched, outlined, and half-written before she began. Her outlines were thorough and determined her chapters. She constructed character biographies and knew their backstories and lineage before writing the first word of the manuscript.

Alex tut-tutted her, his glare piercing.

Maybe he has a point. Maybe I do work more than I realize . . .

She looked around at the elegant but simple furnishings of her home and tried to see it through Alex's eyes. The polished glass and chrome gleamed. The crystal lights were bright. The sleek black lines of the ultra-modern furniture highlighted and complimented the floor-to-ceiling windows overlooking the city and Central Park.

Her office boasted the best natural lighting and floor-to-ceiling bookshelves that held her writing craft tomes and inspirations arranged alphabetically. Sleek mirrored doors hid them from view because they'd ruin the look if exposed. The books were dogeared and showed signs of regular use.

Alex pointed to the windows. "Your view's wonderful from here, but when was the last time you looked at it? Have you even noticed the season changed?" He pointedly peered at her out-of-season warm fuzzy socks and her plush pastel PJs covered with eggs and bunny print. "What good does a penthouse view do you if you're always looking at a computer screen?"

Paige pouted. "I look at the view." To prove it, she hazarded a look out the window. "From time to time."

The sun spread its light over the trees, highlighting their changing colors. It looked like God had tossed a tropical fruit salad with the colors of apricot, watermelon, and lime leaves. Some sun-kissed lemon-yellow leaves looked almost onion-paper thin. *It's gorgeous out there. Time in nature could be inspiring . . . I might need to get outside. Feed my muse, invigorate my mojo.*

"Have you eaten anything today? Had breakfast? Lunch?" Alex's tone reminded her of a principal scolding a kid.

She cringed when she thought of the *Almond Joy* candy bar that had passed for lunch. *Maybe I am hungry.*

Alex was yammering on about food when Tiny began to circle. Alex headed for the door, grabbed Tiny's leash, and called over his shoulder, "It's time you at least visit Central Park. Why have a view of it when you never look, never go? Sadly, your dog spends more time there than you do."

Paige glared at him, refusing to become defensive. "My books don't write themselves. May I remind you, I started the Glam Rom genre, and I must work to afford this view."

She made sure her tone indicated she wasn't happy with the conversation and gritted her teeth. She had nothing to defend. After all, she was on the sunny side of fifty, and Alex was just shy of thirty. *For frick's sake, I could be his mother! Who's he to chastise me?*

Alex looked at her as he opened the door. "How 'bout I

pick you up a bowl of perfection from Pierre's with some crusty warm bread if you use that fancy-dancy shower and put on some fabulous outfit? If your fans could see you now, they'd flip. You have an image to maintain, girlfriend. After all, you are the Queen of the Glitz genre."

"Glam Rom," she muttered, but he didn't appear to be listening.

After the door shut behind him, Paige did as Alex suggested. She caught a whiff of her rumpled PJs as she removed them. *Eww. Alex is right. I'm ripe.* She deposited the clothes in the hamper and assembled her choice of bath oils and scented candles. *Why not go the whole hog?* She poured herself some bubbly and climbed into her free-standing white marble tub.

She had to admit, her state-of-the-art bathroom was wonderful and larger than some people's entire walk-up apartment. She lived in the lap of luxury with a cook, a housekeeper, a masseuse, and a manicurist, who all came to her apartment. Yet she was living like someone in the third world.

Alex brought up a good point. Why have it all when she never experienced it?

She dimmed the starburst crystal chandelier that hung dramatically in the center of the room. Plush pink towels hung at the ready on their heated racks. *Why am I acting like a struggling artist? Something's off with me. And my frickin' brain still hurts.*

Her thoughts tossed to and fro, not landing for long on any one thing. They flitted from one scenario to another, robbing her of peace and quiet and adding to her fierce migraine. She set the jacuzzi to the Lazy River setting and let the scented water flow over her.

Paige mused as she soaked. She had been writing for a long time and generally loved it. Thoughts would flow, images would build, and scenes cascaded from her outline. Yet she couldn't nail down precisely what was bugging her, and that was a problem. Her work in progress, WIP, was . . . well, progressing, and she had met her ten-thousand-a-day word count.

Word in the publishing world had it that her nemesis, Molly Made, wrote fifteen thousand words a day, but Paige didn't buy it. How could that be done? Especially when Molly was a well-known pantser and didn't even know what the hell she was going to write until she sat at her computer. Gossip had it that Molly just sat down, and bingo, words emerged. *Give me a break. How can an author who writes by the seat of her pants get in fifteen thousand words a day?*

A writer's medium was words, and it was a rare event when Paige couldn't get them down on paper, which usually only happened when she had a headache. The problem wasn't her WIP plot, the setting, the characters, or the scenes. But what was? She sank back in her tub, looked out at the night skyline of the cityscape, and drew on her intuition. Her writing wasn't the issue. Something *else* was.

Hmm, maybe the source of my discontent is me. *My life. Not my writing. Not my career.* That was going great guns with no barriers standing in her way. She kept a spiral-bound journal to jot down ideas if revisions or inspiration struck. When it did, she was known to get out of bed and rush to her laptop computer to alter her outline, but that was extremely rare. *No, my muse is fine. It's me.*

The thought drove her out of her tub.

Paige wrapped a thick towel around herself and looked down at her body. *It's not bad, still passable.* There was a little more to her now. *More to love.* A sudden epiphany had her dropping the towel to lay in a puddle at her feet. She stepped over it, wrapped her wet head in another towel, and stood staring at the mirror in shock. *There's more of me to love but* no one to love me. She was the Queen of Romance, yet she had no *hero*, no *king*, no *mate*, no *man* in her life at all.

She pulled herself together and got dressed, selecting an asymmetrical ribbed blush pink brushed cotton crop top with matching wide-cut pants. She could go out or stay in wearing the outfit. If her fans saw her, she'd be lookin' fine as wine.

Her thoughts continued conjuring heroes, wondering how she had neglected to get one for herself. That was her problem in a nutshell. Her work proved she knew the logistics of what to do to find him.

Hmm, Which trope would I use if plotting my own love story? She walked over to her silver-gray crushed velvet chaise, moved the precisely placed silver scatter pillows, and sank into it, thinking hard.

Friend to lover? *Uh no.*

Ned, my editor? She giggled. *Impossible. He's married.*

Anton? *He's gay.*

Cute meet-up? *Risky and iffy.*

Enemy to lover? *Molly Made is my nemesis but female, and I'm straight.*

Billionaire? *Don't need the moola.*

Boss and office manager? *Don't have one . . . Besides, that'd be harassment.*

This is hopeless. She was clueless as to what trope would produce her ideal hero. She sighed with relief when Alex returned, holding a bag with Piere's signature emblem prominently featured. The aroma made her stomach growl.

She stood, stretched, and followed Alex to the dining room table, where he removed cartons from the bag. He walked to the sideboard, retrieved a china bowl, and poured the French Onion soup with melted cheese into it, sliding a plate under to catch any droplets.

He placed the bowl on the table, and with a flourish and a bow, he pulled her chair out. "Madame, have a seat. Bon Appetit."

She sat, thanking him, sipped a spoonful of soup, and moaned. "Oh My God! This *is* perfection on a platter."

He winked. "Told ya, did I not? Be sure you eat every drop. I will see you tomorrow." He gave Tiny a scratch behind the ears and left.

She finished her meal. She retreated to her lounge chair and grabbed her laptop from the low table. After an intense amount of time thinking, she popped up like bread in a toaster, seriously unsetting the throw cushions. She would carefully follow her writing process, like always, plotting her *Find a Man* plan by beginning with an outline. She clicked the Outline tab and started typing.

Goal: Independent Type A woman author wants a hero.
A. Where to find one?
1. Dating sites
2. Speed dating
3. Matchmaker
4. Church
5. Grocery Shopping
6. Chance
B. Motive?
1. A date
2. A mate
3. A spouse
4. A chance to fall in love
C. Possible conflict?
1. Dependence, emotional, financial.
2. Geography, global, USA, state
3. Flexibility
4. Common Interests
5. Compatibility
6. Religion

Paige sighed when her list started getting too long. *None of my characters go through all this planning rigmarole. Heck, it's easy for them. I make it all come together like magic.* There was no magic in her outline except falling in love. She summarized her outline, boiling it down to the simplest concepts. New plan . . .

Find Mr. Right

Fall in Love
Marry
Have Children
Get a Dog

She had the career of her dreams. It was time to find the man of her dreams. The irony was not lost on her. Romance was her livelihood but not part of her life. *I'm ready to find my hero. It's go-time.*

Then she took a look outside. Night had crept in while she was off in her own world. In a true Scarlett O'Hara fashion, she reminded herself that tomorrow was another day.

CHAPTER TWO: EGGS FLORENTINE

Paige awoke the next morning filled with purpose. She showered, blow-dried her hair, then donned a deep burgundy silk lounge set. She exited the bedroom through what she called her Loretta Young French doors. She called them that because she'd seen Loretta Young elegantly emerge from double doors of the same style in an old TV show. Doing her own version, Paige made her dramatic exit from the bedroom to the second-floor balcony overlooking the Great Room.

Alex came through the front door, returning from walking Tiny. "Your mail came. Fredrick, the doorman, had it ready when we came back in." He laid Tiny's leash on the small acrylic entry stand. "Most of it is probably junk, but there's an intriguing brochure in here somewhere. Check it out."

Paige descended the black free-floating staircase, walked into her office, and sat at her desk, adjusting her ergonomic chair. She turned on her computer and clicked on her renamed *Find Mr. Right* document, reviewing what she had typed and reading through all the tweaking and editing she had done before settling on the simple plan.

Alex followed her into the office and handed her the mail.

Paige flipped through the pile and sighed. *So much for a paperless world.* She found the brochure Alex mentioned. The paper stock was quality, and the view it depicted was breathtaking. It featured a charming turn-of-the-century renovated lodge that boasted state-of-the-art amenities, including the Spa Haus, the Boutique Space, an Apothecary, and a large gazebo for on-site entertainment. The background showed the most beautiful mountains in full autumnal perfection within the Great Smoky Mountain National Park.

The Sugarlands Lodge, run by the famed Weathers Girls, boasted authentic regional cuisine and charming cabins. The brochure listed several activities visitors could schedule for additional entertainment, like renowned Appalachian Story-telling, a resident psychic, and best of all, a real-life mountain matchmaker.

Paige's interest was piqued. She decided Sugarlands Lodge would be the perfect place to start her search for *Mr. Right.*

She smiled at Alex, who sat on the other side of the desk with Tiny settled by his feet. "Alex, would you call Sugar-lands Lodge and schedule a week-long reservation as soon as possible for me?" She handed him the brochure. "And get the low down on the place, things not covered in the pamphlet."

Before she headed off on a vacation, she wanted to make sure she was resort-ready. First stop, the pharmacy for her yearly flu shot and COVID booster. A world-class resort town could spawn worldwide health issues, and she wanted to be prepared.

She spent the next several hours working on her WIP and chatted with her editor on a conference call. Alex interrupted her a few times to make sure she ate something. By late evening, she decided she needed to get some sleep.

The next morning, Paige woke at sunrise, as she did every morning. Her appointment at the pharmacy was set for eight o'clock, which was perfect because it gave her plenty of time to get ready.

She dressed in a cutout shoulder tunic over patterned leggings, topped with a deep red shawl. She grabbed her handbag, checking that her phone was within its easy-to-reach front pouch, then slipped her vaccine card in front of the phone so she would have to fish through the larger part of the bag to find it. She grabbed her keycard, told Tiny to stay, and headed for the elevators.

Fredrick tipped his hat when he saw her walking across the lobby. He looked smart and courtly in his doorman uniform. She chitchatted with him briefly, and he held the door as she exited the building.

It was a short walk down Fifth Avenue to the pharmacy. She walked into the pharmacy's Minute Clinic, checked in, and was directed to a chair across from the strategically placed screen that provided privacy for the inoculations.

Paige looked around the empty waiting area. That was until a tall well-built man with a bit of salt and pepper in his hair strode past her and took a seat.

She spent a moment appreciating his broad shoulders, sturdy build, and ... *A ponytail tied at the nape of his neck! What's up with that?* She tilted her head, considering him. For some reason, he stoked her curiosity. He'd make a good hero in one of her novels. How would she cast him? A captain of industry? A movie mogul? An entertainment lawyer?

Hmmm. It didn't matter, the man was hot as hell.

He wore a manly burgundy leather vest open over a tailored shirt with the top few buttons open and cuffs rolled fashionably. His pants were pressed black denim, and his feet sported tasseled loafers. He was a study in contrasts and wore his clothes like they were tailored just for him. He began rolling up his sleeve as he waited.

The pharmacist came out to usher one of them through the half-screen section.

Mr. Hot Dude gestured at her. "Ladies first."

Paige smiled. "Thank you, sir."

She hadn't contracted COVID or the flu even though New York City teemed with people from all over creation, which was why she maintained her yearly boosters. In minutes, she received her shots and colorful bandages, then returned to her chair to wait the mandatory fifteen minutes in case there was an adverse reaction. She'd had no problems with previous injections and expected none now.

Hot Dude stood and muttered, "Here goes nuthin'."

Is he talking to me? Paige wasn't sure.

The shot gal gave the man a wink as she directed him behind the partition.

Flirty bitch.

"Have a seat," the girl said. "Do you want your annual flu shot today, too?"

His voice boomed in the small confines of the cubicle. "Might as well get it over with."

Paige noticed the technician standing just past the edge of the partition. She had the syringe loaded and was set to deliver the jab.

She heard the man say, "I hate —"

Suddenly, there was a loud crash followed by a thud and the aluminum folding chair hitting the floor with a clatter. The man's feet and legs showed beneath the screen. Mr. Hot Dude was on the floor and apparently out cold.

The girl yelled, "He's fainted. Mr. Turner! Mr. Turner!"

Paige jumped up, ready to help. She checked the guy's pulse. It was steady. "Quick. Give him the shots while he's out." She demanded. "He'll need ice for his head. Maybe some OJ."

The girl was younger than Paige and looked a bit panicked. Maybe she had never seen a grown man faint before, but she did as she was told.

The man roused but appeared ashen and drained. Paige remained calm, watching closely as he stirred.

He opened his baby blues and simply said. "I hate needles," as if nothing had happened. He stayed cool and calm as if fainting was an everyday event. No big thing.

Paige just looked at him. "I see that. The good news is, you

were vaxed while you were out, but you may have a headache." She peered into his drop-dead gorgeous eyes, and her
breath stopped briefly. "Pupils normal. I don't think you're
concussed." She extended her hand to pull him upright and
nearly fainted herself as they touched and an electric zing shot
up her arm.

A flush stole over his face, staining his cheeks. "That's a
first."

She quirked a brow. "That was your first COVID vaccina-
tion?"

"No. It's the first time I fainted."

When the pharmacist's assistant returned with saltines, a
cold pack, and bottled orange juice, he waved her off. "I don't
need that."

"Better drink the juice, at least," Paige said. "Or munch a
cracker? Maybe your blood sugar is low."

His brow ticked. "Are you a doctor?"

"Not exactly, but I'm familiar with the basics."

The medic checked him out using a penlight and stetho-
scope. "Better wait a little longer than fifteen minutes. We'll
ice your head. You have a lump forming."

"That makes me a first-class lunkhead, I'd bet."

They all gave a small laugh.

Paige hung around during his *recovery*. "You may need
something to eat. There's a bistro around the corner. You up
for a bite?"

His eyes twinkled. "Maybe a breakfast pastry."

Is he flirting with me? She flashed a smile. "Add some tea,
and it sounds perfect."

They left the drugstore and walked to the bistro. Once they
were seated at a small round table covered with a checkered
linen tablecloth, Paige checked the guy out and noticed him
doing the same thing—checking her out. The morning sun

slanted through the window, providing a bright and cheery ambiance. They hadn't waited long before the server approached them armed with a device to take their order.

When the server left, her companion looked at her with a gleam still twinkling in his eyes. "So, tell me, *are* you a doctor?"

Paige laughed. "Sorta."

His glance turned razor-sharp. "How can you be a sorta doctor? You either are or you aren't."

She shot back. "Are you a lawyer? "

"Kinda."

She smirked. "You either are or you aren't."

He laughed. "Touché"

Paige straightened in her chair. "I earned my doctorate, and part of my studies included hospital rounds and shadowing medical personnel. It comes in handy occasionally in my work and outside it."

"I see. What do you do for a living?" He tilted his head. "You look familiar. Have we met?"

She laughed, then winked. "To answer your first question, I'm a writer."

"What genre?"

"Glam Rom. Romance." She looked at him over her Eggs Florentine. "Your turn. What do you do?"

He squinted, shooting her an odd look. "I'd tell you, but—"

She whispered, "Then you'd have to kill me?"

He smirked. "No, but you might murder me."

Paige looked him straight in the eyes. "Why would I do that?"

"Conflict of interest," he answered. "I may dabble at writing every now and then." He quickly changed the topic back to her. "From what you've told me, can I presume you are Paige A. Newhart? Author of *Celebrity MD*?"

She frowned but kept her tone casual. "Among other titles. That's me. And that's a bad thing?"

"No, that's a wonderful thing," He paused. "For you."

"But not for—"

"Anyone else who writes. Competition." He paused, leaning back in his chair and appraising her before he drawled, "If I was a betting man, I'd have bet you were a dancer."

She shot him a hard glare. "I am."

"Ah, I'm not surprised, you're a real show-stopper."

She laughed. "Thank you, I think. Is that shorthand for an exotic dancer?" She squinted at him. "Like a Las Vegas showgirl?"

His remark gave her pause. *Should I be offended? Or flattered?* She leaned forward, interested in his reply and hating that she cared. *Who gives a shit what he thinks? It's only his opinion.* Then she remembered she was looking for a mate, not just a date. *Yikes!*

He interrupted her mental tirade. "If you're asking if I think you strip for a living, I don't. But do you?"

Paige laughed again. "Hardly. Improv. Modern dance. My height makes classical ballet a no-go." Her brow furrowed. "A man once told me you either have it or you don't."

He grinned.

She raised her Earl Grey tea and asked, "Have you ever read *Celebrity MD*?"

His gaze was direct, and he spoke with certainty in his tone. "Of course. I make a point to read the best sellers. It's important."

Usually, she'd be thrilled to hear that, but her Spidey senses were on alert. "Oh?"

"I'm a writer, too. I make it my business to read my competition. Get to know the enemy."

"Cool." After a beat, it hit her. *Wait. What? Competition? Enemy? Isn't that how you think, girlfriend?* She frowned. "There's plenty of readers out there. Varied audiences. What do you write? Action thrillers?"

"Among other things."

She laughed. "You're hedging. What things?"

"Ever hear of Molly Made?"

She nodded. "The top seller? My nemesis? My arch-rival? Money Molly? Who cleans up rather nicely?" She rubbed her fingers like a stereotypical money changer in a marketplace. "Who hasn't? Of course, I've heard of her. She's a recluse. No one has ever seen her. Not even an author's portrait at the end of her books. It's her shtick, and quite successful if you ask me."

"Why don't you tell me how you really feel?" His tone sounded dry.

She looked up from her delicious egg dish, somewhat startled. "What's the big deal?"

"Oh, I don't know . . . maybe your choice of words." Irony rang in his voice. "*Nemesis* is a pretty strong word, wouldn't ya say?"

She shrugged. "Comme ci, Comme ça. "

"Be that as it may, you saved my life. Rescued the hero of this story."

"Story?"

He waved his finger back and forth between them. "You and me."

She raised a brow in question.

He went on, "An old Chinese saying—"

Paige held up a hand. "Yeah, yeah . . . Save someone's life, and you are responsible for them."

He winked. "For life."

She choked on her tea. "Who are you then?"

"Name's Booker M. Turner, pleased to meet you. And you are . . ."

She hmphed. "You already guessed, though I'm most

likely just a page-turner of yours. I write under my name. Paige A. Newhart."

"What's the A stand for?"

She quickly shot back, "What's the M stand for?"

He sat back at ease and drawled, "It's a mystery. But if you promise not to tell . . ."

Paige raised her right hand. "I promise."

"Maximilian. I use a nom de plume for my books. Chances are you've already read something of mine and don't know it."

"Hmm. Intriguing. Give me a hint. Or at least a title."

"Nope. Where's the fun in that? I like to keep things simple and unremarkable."

She searched his face, wondering why the mystery.

Their waiter stopped at their table and asked, "Can I get you folks anything else?"

Paige shook her head and looked at her watch. "Heavens, where did the time go? I'd love to continue this conversation, but I have to meet Ned soon."

"Oh? The plot thickens. Ned? Your husband? Significant other? Partner?"

She shook her head and smiled. "My ed."

"You call him your *Ed*? Must be some kinda —"

She laughed outright. "No, he's my *ed*, as in editor."

He smiled. "Not a romantic rival then."

Paige hesitated, looking down at her ringless finger and loathing to admit it. "No, I'm married . . .

He quirked a brow and drawled, "You're either married or you're not."

"What I mean is . . . I'm married — not to a brilliant hunk like in my novels — but to my *work*. Haven't found time for a love life. What about you?"

He raised his coffee cup and touched it to hers in a toast. "The same. Smitten but not bitten."

"Ha! What's with us?" Paige sat back in her chair and began to gather her things.

Their waiter presented the check in its leather folder and stood there waiting.

Paige snatched the folder. "Ladies first." She winked at Booker and inserted enough cash to cover their meals and a nice tip. "This has been lovely, but I do have to run."

She stood, and Booker got up to help her with her shawl. It had slipped to the floor when she first sat, and he retrieved it. His fingers brushed the nape of her neck as he placed it on her. The fire he generated within her roared through her veins. *Yowser.*

A bit flustered, she stepped back, putting space between them, all too aware of his touch. "Nice meeting you."

Booker nodded. "It was a pleasure. Let's do this again." He looked at her phone while reaching for his. "How 'bout we exchange our numbers?"

"Sure." Paige searched his face. "You sure you're okay now?"

"Just keep me away from needles, and I'm the original Marlboro Man."

She chuckled. "I think he died of cancer. For your sake, I hope you fare better than him. You look like you've recovered your groove." She waggled her fingers. "Bye-bye."

CHAPTER THREE: OOPS, RINSE AND RE-PEAT

The day was sunny, with just a hint of chill in the air. Paige's editor's office was a hop, skip, and jump from the bistro, so walking was no problem. She reached the impressive skyscraper and pushed through the revolving door.

She took the elevator to the top floor, where her publisher's offices were located. A smartly dressed receptionist greeted her as she entered the office and started to rise.

Paige waved her efforts away. "No need to escort me. I know the way." She breezed through the frosted glass door to Ned's office like a rock star and flashed him a smile.

Ned rose from his sleek, uncluttered desk. He ushered her to the ultra-deluxe grouping of Hollywood Regency furniture that was comfortable despite its ornate gloss. Next to the seating area was a serviceable dry bar that featured crystal decanters and barware. His workspace and desk sat kitty corner to the huge floor-to-ceiling windows. The spectacular view competed with the internal elegance of his office and the power of the solid man — a happily married man.

Paige moved toward him, exchanging air kisses. *Wish I could focus on Ned, not Booker. Down, girl.*

Ned handed her cold sparkling water in a Waterford Lismore tumbler. "How's your WIP goin'?"

Paige wrinkled her nose, accepted the glass, and sat with her legs crossed. "It's happening. Slowly."

Ned sat across from her and shook his head. "That's not

like you. I presume you've outlined it to its most minute detail, so what gives?"

Paige shrugged. "Dunno exactly." She could hardly explain to Ned that she needed to find a spouse. "I'm off my game."

He jumped up. "Speaking of *off*, let me send your flight data now while I'm thinking of it."

"What are you talking about? I thought this meeting was just a touch-base deal. What flight info?"

Ned tilted his head, looking like he couldn't believe what he heard. "For the convention? The National Writers Association Southern Division Soirée—the NWASDS—in Gatlinburg? You'll fly into McGee-Tyson Airport, and you're booked for a suite at the Parkton. That's right, right?

Paige balked. "What? Shit! The conference with the Writers Triad Challenge, WTC? I forgot all about it—I was going to take a much-needed vacation . . ."

"How could you possibly forget? It's the perfect venue to promote your brand. Elyse—with her type A-plus personality—scheduled you for the three-tiered concurrent tracks. You know, the conference, writers' month-long retreat, and the WTC? *You're* scheduled as the Keynote Speaker!"

"Yikes! How can I do all that?"

"The conference tracks are concurrent with additional time built in as needed. This schedule permits conference attendance, participation, and time to write. That's the whole point of a month-long retreat. The Keynote Address kicks the whole caboodle off. This format is perfect for your brand."

She started to nod, then glared at Ned. "Wait. Did you say *I'm* the keynoter? What the hell am I talking about?"

His face revealed his astonishment. "You're talking glitz, blitz, and glamour. As you always do. Make sure it's spicy hot. A lot is riding on this."

Paige groaned and lowered her face into her hands.

"Pardon my senior moment. Elyse is preggers and probably suffers from baby brain or something. Alex isn't up to speed yet."

"Alex? Who's he?"

"My dog walker."

Ned looked surprised. "As far as I know, you don't have a dog."

"I do now. Ever since Tex graced me with his unexpected presence."

Ned scratched his head and looked perplexed. "Tex? Alex?"

"It's a long story."

"Uh-huh . . ."

Paige pulled out her phone and sent Alex's contact info to Ned. "Send the flight details to Alex."

"The dogwalker?"

"He's been promoted. He's become my new assistant. Shoot, there's the matter of one little itty-bitty detail . . . Tiny."

"What's that?" He shook his head. "Never mind. This office can take care of any details for you. Allen can—"

"Alex."

"Whatever." Ned moved to his desk, sat in his designer chair, put his elbows on the glass, and ran his large hands through his thick hair, messing it up royally. He looked at her, his patience diminishing before her eyes. "A tiny detail isn't a problem. We can deal. No need to sweat the small stuff."

Paige stood in front of the desk. "Tiny *is* the detail, Ned. He's a dog of unknown—at least to me—pedigree."

"Is he a pocket pooch or a handbag tiny cutie? That's no biggie. Airlines deal with celebrity dogs all the time."

She hastened to explain. "That's what I thought from his name, but Tex has a sense of humor. Tiny is humongous. Did I mention he's a mutt? Kinda looks like part Belgian Sheepdog and part Scooby Doo."

"I'm sure Andrew —"

"Alex."

"Whatever. It's his problem now. I'll alert Rosalie to be ready to step in, just in case."

"Hm, Miss Designer Clothes may be out of her depth where Tiny's concerned, ya know?"

Ned groaned. "Whatever. Between Anthony —"

"Alex."

"Whatever. Between him and Rosalie, we'll figure it out. Wait. Tex is a war correspondent, how did he end up with a mutt to begin with? He's always on call or an assignment. He doesn't need a dog."

"Tex is a big teddy bear. A real softie. He rescued him from Ukraine . . . and now Tiny's my problem until Tex's gig is up. And believe me, having Tiny live with me is like being a tiny bit pregnant."

Ned moaned audibly and buried his head deeper into his hands. Again. "I have a headache."

Paige snorted. "Tell me about it. I've had a doozy of one for the last several days."

Ned straightened. "Whatever. Maybe this writer challenge will get you going on your next manuscript."

Paige sighed. "When did you say this convention begins?"

"Next week."

"Holy Shit!" Paige sprang up. "I've got to get outta here!" She quickly gathered herself and her things to leave.

Ned stopped her and said, "You don't seem to get how important it is to keep your brand fresh. Trust me, this is a good move."

"Screw my brand. And send all that information to Alex."

His glance pierced her as he grumbled, "You're welcome."

As she rode the elevator to the lobby, visions of another man stole into her head. That man appeared to be Booker.

It was very quiet when Paige got home. *Alex must be walking Tiny.* Neither of them could be considered the silent type. She headed upstairs to her bedroom. Apparently, Alex had received Ned's info, because her luggage lay open on the bed, partially filled with some of her clothes.

She opened her walk-in closet and toed off her ankle boots, placing them in their proper spot. When she turned to grab her furry bunny slippers, they were not where they should be. *Hmm, I always keep everything in its place. I have a sneaking suspicion that Tiny knows where they are.* She picked up her fur-lined boots and slipped them on her feet. They were the next best thing to her slippers.

She scanned her bedroom, spotting some fluff here and other stuff there. In fact, tuffs of faux fur and other bits of what had once been her slippers formed a trail. It didn't take much of a detective to uncover that Tiny was indeed the culprit behind the missing slippers.

She ground her teeth." Grrreat. Just great."

A few minutes later, the patter of doggy nails on her hardwood floors and pungent wet mutt odor preceded the appearance of the bouncing dog. Tiny bulldozed into her bedroom and nearly knocked her down with his ruckus and rowdy greetings.

Alex entered the bedroom a minute later, informing her she needed to choose between the red ensemble or the sleek charcoal asymmetric dress for her keynote address.

She had to admit that Alex knew what he was doing.

Alex pursed his lips. "You need to pack whatever you sleep in, boss lady. Your lingerie is up to you, too. Those things I do not deal with. I've done my due diligence and packed everything for hot weather and cold, but I draw the line at packing your undies and sundries. By the way, I notice you wear a lot of Donna Karan, so I packed the Seven."

Paige giggled. "Who are you, and what have you done

with my dogwalker? The Seven Easy Pieces? That's so nine-teen-eighties."

Alex laughed. "Yes, ma'am, but the transforming day wear to evening wear concept still works today. By the way, I included your Donna Karran blue stack-sequin gown for the Fairy Tale Masquerade Ball. And your Ralph Lauren autumn plaid fringe poncho for the cooler nights. This isn't my first rodeo, sugar. I have six sisters and learned from the best." He stood by the bed, packing the shoes she tossed him. "I've been a personal assistant before, and something about the poor little rich girl thing you've got goin' on cries out to me."

Alex looked up to see her gaping at him. "What? I read your books. But getting back to the convention . . . Sunny Days, Co-owner —"

"Wait. What? Sunny Days? That's her real name?"

Alex crossed his heart and held up his hand. "Yep. She married into the Days clan."

"That sounds like something I'd cook up in one of my novels."

He chuckled. "Anyhoo, as I was saying . . . I made arrangements with Sunny Days for me and Tiny. Fortunately, the Lodge has an exemption for pets. I have some stuff to tend to here, but I've got things for Tiny well in hand. He gets a trip to the vet to bring him into compliance with the Lodge and airline policies, and I made arrangements for his cargo crate. All you have to do is remember to retrieve him from the airport. A courtesy van will transport you both to the Lodge. I'll fly in as soon as I wrap things up so I can be there for Tiny . . . and you. Lord knows you need my brand of help."

You're telling me. Then she frowned, remembering the suite Ned had booked for the conference.

As if reading her mind, Alex said, "You were booked at the Parkton in Gatlinburg, but they can't meet your, uh, complex needs. "

"My complex needs?"

Alex double-checked the packing. "Uh-huh, Tiny. Sugarlands Lodge welcomes pets. Remember that brochure? You were planning a vacay there anyway. It meets your needs with its resident psychic, masseuse, and matchmaker. It's a much better place for you. Methinks it will help you land a man. Heaven knows you need one. A real macho man. You're restless and headachy, and you know you need to get laid. You know I'm right, girl, I got your number, so be on the lookout."

She threw Alex a look. "Who are you? Dr. Freud?"

She hated to admit it, but she had arrived at the same conclusion. *But I think I've already found my man at the pharmacy.* "Set me up for all those activities you mentioned, will ya. Please?"

She moved to her lingerie drawer and said over her shoulder, "Add hiking boots and jeans, too. I might want to do some exploring and figure things out in Mother Nature's backyard."

"Done and done. I'm good at this. I did my Smoky Mountain research and packed accordingly. And those appointments are arranged. By the way, I like that description of the great outdoors. You must be a writer. How about Mom Nature's cradle."

She giggled. "Hmm. *Cradle?* That's a good one. You must be a writer's assistant."

Alex grinned, and damned if her cheeky mutt didn't give her a toothy doggy smile as well. Tiny brought Paige his favorite toy — a droopy furry rabbit — and dropped it at her feet.

Paige chuckled. "Sorry, boy. Can't play now, but who needs a cookie, huh? Who does? How about a nice big chew bone?"

Tiny bounded out of the room in search of his raw bone.

Paige retreated to her chaise, grabbed her laptop, and using a remote, lit her ribbon fireplace set in the wall along the way. She stretched out and turned on her computer. *I'd better plot my glitz and glam keynote address. Ned's right about the writing challenge. I've been looking for more tangible ways to give back.*

She had reached a point in her career life to offer a hand-up to aspiring authors. Her tribe and the writer's guild she belonged to had helped her along the way.

She texted Alex.

Need flight deets.

K

Alex came in and handed her a mug of hot hard cider. His phone pinged, and he replied to whatever message he received.

She jolted upright in a sudden panic. "Tiny! What am I going to do with him while I'm at the conference? You . . . won't be there . . . and I can't leave him alone in the room."

"Cool your jets, girlfriend, I got ahold of the concierge, Sunny Days—"

"Wait. I thought you said she's the co-owner."

Alex gave her a reassuring smile. "Sunny wears many hats, and she said she's got it covered." He grinned. "Now, about your gown for the Fairy Tale Masquerade Ball—"

Paige shook her head. "I don't have time for that stuff."

"You told me about your *Find Mr. Right* plan. This is a necessary step. Don't worry about a thing. I'll be like one of Disney's little mice and get you into a Cinderella get-up."

Paige nodded. "Whatever. But do me a favor. Make sure Tiny's chipped and has my contact info on his collar." She winked. She lifted her hand to cover her heart, promising, "I'll do my best to find my Cinderfella, too."

The week flew by quickly, and the next thing Paige knew, she was in the air flying to McGee Tyson Airport in eastern Tennessee. She wondered if Booker would be at the conference. He'd been on her mind quite a bit since their drugstore encounter and had already been added as a welcome candidate in her hunt for Mr. Right. *Wonder what he writes? Didn't he say he just dabbles in writing? He didn't say what genre, though. He looks like he has his adventures goin' on in his brain. Has he published? A name like Booker oughta make him a shoo-in for publication.*

Paige relaxed in her first-class seat and sipped her champagne. Alex had her luggage sent ahead, so all she had to do was retrieve Tiny from the cargo. She had a collapsible leash in her bag.

She leaned back and closed her eyes. *Wonder what I'll find in the Smokies? Will I discover the man of my dreams? Or another headache?*

CHAPTER FOUR: A CIRCLE

The pong of the airplane's PA system jolted Paige awake, which shocked her. She normally didn't nap during flights. Naps always made her feel sluggish. *That's why I avoid them like an icy sidewalk. Not that I would mind falling into Booker's arms if I slipped.*

The flight crew scurried, moving from seat to seat, collecting garbage and retrieving drinks, glasses, and cans. The crew's next pass urged passengers to return their seats to the upright position and stow their trays, indicating the flight was almost over. As everyone shifted to comply, the pilot confirmed their final approach to the airport.

A short time later, the captain spoke again. "Cabin crew, please take your seats for landing."

Clicking seatbelts from surrounding cabin mates reminded Paige to tighten her own. Strong suggestions from the airline industry advised passengers to always wear them when seated, and based on recent airline mishaps, news reports reinforced the wisdom of complying. Paige generally relied on and followed such guidelines.

She felt the slowing of the aircraft, then heard the groan of deceleration and the release of the landing gear. It wasn't long before the wheels hit the runway, accompanied by a hop and bounce and then the protesting screams of the engines as the plane rolled down the runway.

Paige winced as the plane finally turned toward the terminal. She often worried they'd plow through the landing dock and terminal, ending in her facing a fiery death. People shifted in their seats, and some disregarded announcements to remain seated as they approached the terminal.

After the plane came to a complete stop, Paige let out a huge sigh of relief. *We made it. Thank God.* She checked with the steward to find where to go to retrieve Tiny.

As everyone waited for the doors to open, the captain announced, "Welcome to McGee-Tyson Airport. Again, thank you for flying with us. The temperature is a balmy sunny 72 degrees. Enjoy your time in the Volunteer State."

Booker M. Turner's writing process consisted of sitting down and writing whatever story popped into his head, which he was told made him a pantser. He had to admit he had never been much of a planner, so it was a godsend to have a personal assistant to take care of all the details for him.

He had Bear secured in her carrier but was running late as usual despite having a car service set to whisk him off to the airport the required two hours early. He was grateful his assistant arranged to ship his luggage off ahead of time, and his trip to the Great Smoky Soirée thingy had been booked months ahead.

Despite having every detail covered, he fumbled at the security gate, having forgotten to wear easy-on, easy-off loafers. He'd also worn a sweater vest and suit jacket, making going through TSA even more cumbersome. They chose to pull him aside to check him further, running the wand over him and Bear. On top of that, they decided to question him further and do an in-depth search of Bear's carrier, rattling him all the more and struggling to keep his cool.

Finally, determining he posed no security threat, TSA waved him off. He wasted more time as he fumbled to re-don his shoes, vest, and jacket as fast as he could. He should never have worn a belt either. *What an effin' nuisance.* Coping with the belt, tying his shoes, refilling his pockets with his keys and loose change, and dealing with Bear was exhausting. *One would think a man with a pocket pooch was an unlikely threat, but nooo.*

The TSA agent did chuckle when he told her his ball of fluff was named Bear. "I didn't want her to feel intimidated and get an anxiety disorder due to her diminutive size, so I over-compensated with her name."

Unimpressed, the hefty TSA agent raised a brow and pursed her lips. "Mm-hmm." Obviously, she had no concept of the angst Bear might experience and no sense of humor to boot.

Finally freed from TSA security, Booker headed to his gate and boarded the plane when his section was called, intending to hold Bear and her carrier on his lap. When the steward came around, she said Bear's carrier had to be stowed beneath the seat directly in front of him. When he stooped to comply, two warning barks came from the carrier next to him, and Bear responded in kind.

The woman seated beside him glared, pointing out that she and her mutt were there first.

The barking cacophony between Bear and her neighbor set the other canines on board barking, drawing unwanted attention.

The steward returned, placing her hands on her ample hips. "Hand her over. That nuisance dog has to be stowed elsewhere." She sighed loudly. "Another hold up."

Booker balked but barked at the woman. "Do you know who you're talking to? Don't you know who I am?"

The steward merely looked at him, lifted the microphone to her lips, and said, "We have a passenger here who doesn't know who he is. Does anyone here know who this man is?"

One passenger called out, "Hey buddy, check your ID."

Booker wasn't amused. He became thoroughly pissed off when he was given a receipt with Bear's name and identification number.

The steward lifted Bear easily — crate and all — and in a stern tone, stated, "You can pick her up at the cargo area when we land."

"I paid good money for her seat," he thundered.

"Uh-huh. Yes, sir, you did. Now you can either let me stow her or be removed from this flight. A disruptive dog goes to the hold."

Booker decided to hold his tongue. He shifted in his seat. "Don't worry, baby Bear, Daddy will get you soon." *What the hell else can go wrong?*

After landing, Paige sailed through the terminal, went where she was directed, and retrieved Tiny. After Tiny nearly knocked her into next week with his pent-up devotion and slobbering welcome, she air kissed her mutt. With a swipe of her hand, she wiped her face and ruffled Tiny's fur, cooing, "Who's the mighty mutt? Hmm?"

Once outside, she opened the crate and clipped the leash on. Finally freed, Tiny lunged ahead, and being the friendly boy he was, Tiny made a beeline for the bit of fluff masquerading as a dog. The tidbit Pomeranian, seeing the big lummox, started racing toward him, yip-yapping and tugging on its lead, too. The two met up, running happy circles around each other and their owners, tangling them royally and drawing them together. Paige, breathlessly trying to control her dog and keep her balance, finally looked up and found herself face-to-face with her drugstore man . . . Booker.

He took one look at her and drawled, "Fancy seeing you here."

Paige smiled, then shot back, "We have to stop meeting like this."

They began untangling themselves from the leashes, and she wrangled with Tiny while asking, "What are you doing here?"

Booker looked at her, his eyes twinkling. "What are *you* doing here?"

Paige burst out. "You first."

He shook his head. "Ladies first."

Paige shot him an exasperated look and had to fight back a smile as she untangled the last of Tiny's leash.

He shrugged. "We need to introduce—"

She looked up. "Huh?"

He smiled and pointed to his squirrely dog. "Bear meet . . ." He waved at Tiny.

Paige struggled not to laugh but failed. "That powder puff is named Bear?"

"Didn't want her to have an inferiority complex. Who's that giant?"

She snickered. "His name is Tiny."

Booker let loose a big belly laugh. "Tiny is a beast!"

She winked. "Good thing we've all had our shots."

Booker laughed again as he straightened out the last of Bear's leash. "What a sight we are. Me with my little mole-hole-sized Bear, and you with a Tiny the size of Mount Everest."

Their dogs sniffed each other's rear ends, and then Tiny licked Bear, knocking her on her side. The little fluff ball jumped back to her feet, tail wagging a mile a minute.

Booker looked bemused. "Will you look at that . . . Tiny's kisses bowled Bear over, and she seemed to like it."

Paige nodded. "Love at first sight? Or should I say, sniff?"

He looked at her with a glint in his eye. "So it appears. What brings you here of all places?"

"I'm attending the NWASDS at the Gatlinburg Convention Center."

"Me too." He smiled then said with a wink, "Looks like we'll be seeing a lot of each other then."

She waved. "See you around."

Booker grinned. "I think these two will make sure of that. See you at the hotel."

Paige put Tiny back into his crate, turned, and noticed a handsome blonde dude standing near a large SUV holding a placard reading *Smithfield*, the name she'd asked them to use so she could remain incognito. She moved toward the guy, nodding at his sign. "Sugarlands Lodge? I'm here. That's me." She waved at the crate. "This is Tiny."

The dude nodded, then loaded the crate with little trouble. "Name's Jesse Days. Right this way." He opened the door for her. "Your luggage arrived this morning and is all set in your cabin."

Paige asked Jesse to drop her off at the Gatlinburg Convention Center before taking Tiny to the Lodge. "I want to get my registration packet and check out the space before the conference begins."

"No problem. Someone can watch Tiny until you get there. It'll take me about an hour or so to get back. That all right?"

"That's fine."

"Excellent. I'll pick you up at this same spot. If you get lost inside, just ask for the Airport Road entrance."

Paige waved him off, followed the signs to the reception area labeled *Author's Lair*, and slipped into line. She found her name tag, speaker's ribbon, and ID tag, then picked up her swag bag. The bags were generally filled with treats and gifts. She wondered what goodies this one held.

She was used to being the one giving out swag, so it was fun to be on the receiving end for once. She took note of the striking purple bag with *Mellow Magic* scrawled in silver across its exterior. The reception area boasted a coffee bar, wine bar, teas, soft drinks, charcuteries, pastries, and a variety of snacks and candy. *Looks like the Author's Lair is nicely prepared with all sorts of amenities to cater to the authors.*

The restful room was decked out in fall splendor, giving

the space a comfortable, homey feeling. The windows were designed for privacy from outside observation but allowed the mountain city scenery to dominate the view.

She decided to peruse the Soirée swag bag's contents later. First, she wanted to view the stage where she'd give her keynote address, then check out the breakout rooms where she'd participate in book signings, author's breakout sessions, and other events.

As the day grew to a close and the setting sun stained the clouds and sky in gold and orange, Paige set out to find the Airport Road Exit and catch her ride to the Sugarlands Lodge.

After Jesse dropped her off at the Lodge, she entered the charming inn and was greeted by an effervescent young springy black-haired moppet inside the Reception Room.

"Hey, welcome. I'm Sunny Days, Social Director, Matchmaker, resident Psychic, and now current receptionist. Pleased to meet you." Then she took a second look. "Oh heavens, the moon must be in the seventh house, all right! You're Paige Newhart!"

Paige took a step back as the monsoon energy of Sunny Days let loose.

"Oh, before I forget, may I have your autograph? I'm your number one fan. And guess what? I'm a writer, too. I even have a pen name, Kathy Kalmar. Oh heavens, you must be here for the NWASDS Conference in Gatlinburg." Sunny giggled and acted like an over-excited fan, and then she gushed, "I love your books, and I think you wrote a great alpha-beta hero in your last book."

Huh? What's an alpha-beta hero? Paige soon found a pen thrust in her hand. *Sunny sure lives up to her name. That's a lot of energy wrapped up in the woman.*

Sunny thrust what looked like a placard at Paige to get her autograph. Paige picked it up and read it aloud.

According to words of lore

In the days of yore,
Those who pass through this cabin door
Will find lasting love evermore.
Tis love y'all find
Of the forever kind.
Two hearts resting here,
For all time, bind.
If two lovers together see the Ghost Stag, united they shall forever
be.
So, mote it be,
As y'all shall see.

"What's this all about?" Paige asked.

"We have a surprising number of single guests who find their true love here and end up leaving engaged."

Paige's brow rose. "Really?"

Sunny nodded. "Yes, it's been happening for generations. In fact, my Gram and Pops were among the first couples who fell in love here, and the rest is history. I got my parents back together here and . . ."

A hard-to-describe look passed over Sunny's face, and she closed her eyes. When she opened them, she looked intently focused, then grabbed Paige's hand. "I can feel it. Wait. There's a match for you here, too. You will meet your match very soon. OMG, I can feel his energy. This *knowing* is part of my gift."

Paige shifted on her feet and said, "Do you mind if I settle in first? What I'd really like is a nice hot—"

"Your wish is my command. I'll reserve an appointment for a massage and jacuzzi experience at the Spa Haus that will blow your mind. The directions are in your cabin, go there, and you'll be all set. Would you like a home-cooked southern dinner served here? I can send one over if you love mouth-watering southern fried chicken."

Almost overpowered by Sunny's energy, Paige replied. "Thank you. How 'bout I autograph my latest book instead of this? Hmm?" She opened her tote, pulled out a copy of *Celebrity MD*, and spoke as she signed the inside cover. "To my most enthusiastic fan, Sunny, with thanks. Enjoy! Paige Newhart, 2024."

Sunny threw her arms around Paige, then jumped up and down.

Jesse walked in with a wry smile and rescued Paige, saying, "I'll take you to your cabin. We'll pass the Spa Haus on our way."

Sunny scowled and then smiled brightly. "Tiny is settled for now, and your assistant called saying he would be here this evening to take over his care. I'll order your dinner and set up your massage for 8:00 p.m. There's only one other appointment, but you'll have your privacy most of the time."

"Sounds good to me. What can go wrong with a soothing massage?"

CHAPTER FIVE: HOTEL SUITE HOTEL

Booker walked to the car rental desk to pick up his *Ford Escalade*, only to be handed the keys for a small sedan. "What happened to my Escalade?"

"Supply chain issues have played havoc with our business. It's a national issue. We're lucky we have anything at all. Demand is sky-high. It takes longer down here. We're not a big city airport, but we're fixin' to become one someday." He splayed his hands and shrugged. "I'm so sorry, but it's all we got."

Booker kept his cool. The young man behind the counter wasn't at fault and couldn't control the situation.

"The per diem cost is less, if that helps, and the tank is full. Do you want it?"

Booker smirked. "Guess I have no choice, unless you rent motorcycles?"

"Afraid not, but there's Orange Jeep Service once you get to Gatlinburg or Pigeon Forge."

Booker said, "I'll take the cheap seat."

The kid winked. "Good choice. Sign here."

"You sure there's no Rent-a-Harley?"

The kid shook his head and chuckled. "Don't think your dog would do well on that ride."

"Bear loves my *Harley*. We ride all the time. She even has her own goggles and helmet."

The boy looked at Bear and roared with laughter. "Seriously?"

Booker grabbed the keys, and Bear yipped.

Folding himself into the pint-sized car was a feat. His knees were nearly up to his chin, and he felt like a giraffe in a clown car. He placed Bear's crate behind him. His irritation grew when the five-inch navigation screen couldn't find the driving directions to his destination, the Summit Hotel. Thankfully, his cell app found the directions, which indicated it'd take almost two hours to reach the hotel. He hoped the amenities there were better than his vehicle.

With growing impatience at his late start, he hit the road, figuring he'd reach his hotel near dusk. When he flicked the radio on and got terrible reception, he growled, making Bear whine. The best way to describe his mood was foul.

To make matters worse, he missed his turn on the winding and narrow road, then he lost cell reception and GPS navigation. *Dammit. Next time, print a copy of the damn driving directions.*

As twilight began, a huge deer darted across the road, and he reacted automatically, turning the wheel and nearly driving off a switchback turn and down an incline. Bear yapped as her crate slid sharply across the back seat.

"Sorry, girl." *This damn road has more curves than Paige.* He shook his head. The woman kept popping into his thoughts, especially after seeing her again at the airport.

When Booker regained his breath and his heartbeat returned to normal, he found himself inside the Great Smoky National Park, passing a sign that said *Elkmont* — wherever that was. He knew where he had been and had no desire to retrace his steps to find out where he had gone wrong, so he continued driving straight ahead, which proved to be a literal long and winding road.

As he maneuvered through another switchback, he checked his phone and saw the GPS navigation working again, directing him toward Gatlinburg and — ironically enough — Airport Road. *Must be on the right track at last.*

Booker breathed a sigh of relief and waded cautiously through the heavy traffic. *What the frick! You got to be kidding me. Are these people cruising?* Pickup trucks boasting both Dixie and United States flags were moving slowly down the boulevard. Teens rode in the truck beds, laughing with music booming from their devices, he assumed. Yeah—Friday. The locals were cruising, while conference attendees and tourists were trying to reach their destination on a balmy autumn night.

When he reached a junction in the road, the GPS directed him to turn onto a road in utter blackness. He felt panicked and fatigued but shrugged. It had to be another entry into the park. After driving a short distance, he spied small lights on a wooden gateway. *That looks like it could possibly be the hotel driveway? I hope so. This drive is getting hairy.*

The GPS finally announced, "Your destination is on the right."

As he drove up the hill, lights pierced the night, and he found himself approaching a portico and safety at last. He parked in front of the hotel, which sat on a summit. Literally, since there appeared to be a drop-off on either side of the structure.

He got out of his rental vehicle, lifted Bear out of her crate, and let her walk on her leash to a patch of mountain grass so she could pee. He hugged Bear when she was done and led her into the surprisingly rustic yet somewhat elegant lobby. Pleased with the warmly inviting interior, he all but crawled in relief to the reception desk.

A well-dressed young man wearing a metal pin reading *Tad* neatly attached to his buttoned black vest greeted him. "Good evening, sir. Welcome to the Summit Hotel." A few seconds later, Tad promptly began sneezing and gasping for breath. His face reddened with the effort to catch his breath.

Another guy rushed to Tad's side and produced an

epinephrine pen, shouting, "You have a pet? Get it outta here. No pets allowed."

Booker scooped up Bear and cursed. Shocked and alarmed at the way the guy was yelling, he blurted. "But I have a reservation."

"Leave. My brother is highly allergic to pet dander. Our father owns this hotel. Wait outside, and I'll help you find other accommodations, but you need to get out of here right *now.*"

Booker grumbled as he complied. Once outside, he sat on the stone wall outlining the hotel frontage to wait. He was shaking, and Bear trembled in his arms. "Who knew you were so dangerous? Guess you must be a grizzly, huh, Bear?" He stroked her fluff, soothing her and calming himself.

Some minutes later, a young woman wearing a similar vest came outside and handed him a printout. "I'm sorry for the unwelcome welcome, but we really can't accommodate pets here. Most of the nearby hotels are completely booked because the leaf peepers are here in droves for the fall foliage and several competing festivals."

Booker half rose from his seat but stayed put when Bear yelped in protest. "So there's no rooms available?"

The desk clerk stretched out a hand to assure him. In a rush, she said, "But I contacted Sunny Days at the Sugarlands Lodge out near Elkmont, and fortunately—because it's out of town and inside the National Park—I was able to get you a reservation." She cast a glance at Bear. "They accept pets and should have a room or a cabin, at least. A cabin might be a good choice for you. Is that okay?" She paused and added, "For your inconvenience with this fiasco, I'll transfer your deposit to Sugarlands Lodge."

He looked down at Bear cuddled into a ball on his lap, still shaking. He released a long sigh, accepting what he could not control, and nodded. "That's fine. Thanks."

She gave a small laugh. "They'll love your small dog. The Lodge is about a ten-minute drive from here. "

"Yes, I know. I passed Elkmont on my way here. Thank you for all you've done. I apologize for my short temper, but my flight from New York was horrendous, the car rental place didn't have the vehicle I'd booked, and the drive here was unnerving."

"Normally—"

Booker held up a hand, fast becoming accustomed to hearing that word. "I know. I get it." He stroked Bear's quivering body.

The woman twisted her hands and began again. "Normally, I'd have someone lead you, but I'm afraid with the emergency, we're understaffed." An ambulance pulled up as she spoke, and medics spilled out of the vehicle, rolling a gurney.

Booker spoke. "Is Tad going to be all right?"

"Probably." She began explaining the route. "Once you get past the Friday night cruisers, it's a straight shot into the park. Turn right at the Visitors Center and then take a left into Elkmont. It's near the campground. If you reach the checkpoint, you've gone too far. The Lodge is on the left. You can't miss it."

Booker cursed softly and muttered, "Wanna bet?" Louder he added, "Got it. Thanks. Come on, Bear, our adventure awaits."

The drive into the deep blackness of the park was nerve-wracking, but at least he knew what to expect since he had driven this way before. Once the GPS made its familiar announcement, he turned and drove his weary ass up the barely lit driveway until he reached the gravel parking lot. Solar lanterns led him to a parking spot near the entrance.

He rubbed his hands over his five o'clock shadow, then

grabbed Bear's carrier, his carry-on suitcase, and the backpack containing Bear's paraphernalia. He entered Sugarland Lodge and headed for the reception desk, barely glancing at the outstanding fireplace and beautifully carved staircase.

A curly-headed, blue-eyed, black-haired beauty greeted him, speaking rapid-fire, barely taking a breath. "Welcome to the Sugarlands Lodge. I'm Sunny Days, and this handsome man" — she hooked her thumb to the man behind her — "is my husband, Jesse. You must be Mr. Turner. You've had quite a night, I hear. Poor Tad. He's so sensitive to pets. They call him a frequent flyer over at Mountain Heritage, our closest hospital out in Sevierville. I don't think you drove through there. But here I am talking up a storm, and you lookin' like you need a rest. I have your room ready. I'm on the night shift and can meet your needs."

Jesse chuckled, and Booker figured he must have raised his brow automatically — too tired to do it deliberately — because the effervescent young woman blushed when she realized what she had just said.

"Um . . . Here's your key. We don't use keycards here. Using old-fashioned keys is what we like to think of as part of our charm. But you don't need me running on and on. How 'bout I send you a hot hard apple cider moonshine to help you relax? Or you could use the Spa Haus hot tub . . . Or I can send for our masseuse —"

He stopped her word tsunami. "That's fine. Thanks. I'll just take you up on your hot hard cider offer and complete the paperwork online, if that's okay with you?"

Sunny nodded. "Sure thing. Follow me." She led him down a rock-strewn and solar-lit footpath. She stopped at the door labeled *Pumpkin Eater* and unlocked it, extending her arm and saying, "Ta-da. Here you are."

Booker released Bear from her carrier, and she ran around the room as if she'd slept all day. Come to think of it, she had slept all day. Bear was in doggy heaven sniffing the river-rock fireplace. When she looked up at him, her white fur chin was covered in soot, making her look like she had a black beard.

Sunny giggled at the sight. "I'll let you settle in and have that cider sent right over."

Booker tried unsuccessfully to clean the soot from Bear's chin. Then he quickly shed his suitcoat, vest, shoes, and keys to stretch out on the bed, spotting a small tent card resting on the nightstand. Curious, he picked it up and read.

According to words of lore
In the days of yore,
Those who pass through this cabin door
Will find lasting love evermore.
Tis love y'all find
Of the forever kind.
Two hearts resting here,
For all time, bind.
If two lovers together see the Ghost Stag, united they shall forever be.
So, mote it be,
As y'all shall see.
Enjoy your stay in 333.

He rolled to his side, replacing the card as he laughed. There was a discrete knock at the door, and he rose to open it and found Sunny Days standing there with a steaming mason jar smelling like apple pie.

She handed him the mug. "Here ya go." She gave him a big smile. "I put you in cabin three-thirty-three."

"So I see."

"That's the Lodge's lucky number. Legend has it if you're single, you won't be by the time you leave." She winked.

"How do you know I'm single?"

"I have a feelin'. I know these things." Her hand moved over her heart. "I feel it here" — her fingers trailed to her gut — "and in here. Word around here is I've got the sight." She winked again. "You know . . . psychic."

"Good for you."

"G'night, Mr. Turner."

Booker just nodded and saluted as she left.

CHAPTER SIX: TOGETHER

Paige glanced at the pamphlets she found in her cabin as she ate the delicious Southern comfort food Jesse had dropped off. She noticed the selection of pamphlets included many that Sunny Days had written about the surrounding Great Smoky Mountain National Park. The tone of the writing was as sunny as its author, describing the attractions and available activities. As she read, she came across useful information about the Spa Haus and remembered that Sunny had already made a massage and jacuzzi appointment for her.

After finishing her meal, she ditched her traveling clothes and replaced them with a lounging outfit for her trip to the spa. The small purple trifold for the Spa Haus listed the hours, indicating it was open until 9:00 p.m. and later by special request. It also had an image of the luxurious jacuzzi. *Just what I'm looking for.*

Paige picked up another pamphlet from the bureau as she surveyed her cabin. She was housed in *Sleeping Beauty*. She smiled. *Don't I wish? What prince will kiss me awake? Hmm, sounds like some consent issues to be considered.* Beside that brochure was another about the American Black Bears that were native to the area. *I'd better read this now — just in case.* She was amazed but relieved to learn they were largely herbivores.

Her thoughts returned to her charming cabin and upcoming speech. She'd already outlined her glitz and glam topics but wondered if she should include them. *But right now, I see en suite is an over-statement.* Unfortunately, the bathroom contained no tub, only a small shower. Instead, guests were encouraged to use the Spa Haus for anything more luxurious.

In the meantime, Paige washed her face using the mauve bar of lavender-scented soap imprinted with the monogram MMA in a French Script font. The purple wrapper bore the words *Mellow Magic Apothecary* written in silver. The soap had a lovely creamy texture and a refreshing fragrance. As she dried her face with the ultra-soft towel, she wondered if she should do some work before going to the spa. *What am I thinking? Of course, I'll work first.*

She fished her computer out of her laptop tote along with her notebook. Although she used her tech tools to outline and write her manuscripts, the notes in her writer's notebook were always written in longhand. She gave the keynote speech a quick read-through, satisfied with what she'd written. *There, mission accomplished. Work's done.*

She closed her notes and unpacked her bags, hanging her outfits before any wrinkles could set in. Her clothes were perky and practical with a splash of fun, festivity, and fabulous. She did enjoy her designer duds. Some even made her look like a romance fashion queen. She'd occasionally pause her writing schedule to indulge in some shopping drama for a change of pace. *Speaking of indulging, it's spa time.*

She stepped outside and stopped, staring at the huge full moon overhead. The news had reported the sky would feature what they coined a *supermoon* because the moon was closer to the Earth. She held her breath, enthralled by the sight, but reminded herself of her appointment and followed the path to the spa.

Outside the Spa Haus, a huge Chinese gong—a recent upgrade, judging by the disturbed surroundings—shone in the moonlight. The gong hung suspended inside a wooden stand that held a mallet, lending an eastern touch to its rustic setting. After passing through the purple door, Paige was thrilled to find an up-to-date spa with purple, lavender, and mauve colors everywhere. A young woman, wearing what must be their signature purple color, emerged from one of the rooms, ambient light casting a purple haze over her. The scent of honey, lilac, and lavender followed the woman. Paige breathed it in, allowing herself to relax and simply chill.

The young woman saw Paige and handed her a towel. "Howdy, y'all must be Miss Smithfield. Wrap this around your head so the oils don't mess with your hair." Then the gal took a second, closer look and squealed, "OMG! Paige Newhart! Well, I never! I declare I didn't put it together that you are *thee* Paige Newhart, best-selling author. Forgive me, I'm yapping like a newborn pup who can't find his mama. You're listed as P. Smithfield." She fanned herself, then recovered and said, "I'm Tully Baker, and I do go on when I'm flustered. I didn't expect *you*. I mean, I expected a patron, but not *you*."

Paige smothered a smile and did nothing to clear up Tully's confusion. *Occupational hazard. Secret identities are secret for a reason.* "Nice to meet you, too. I presume you want me to come inside so you can get to work on me."

"Good Golly, Miss, er Smithfield, yes. I'll step out for a minute so you can undress. Just place your things in that wicker basket over yonder, and I'll get Miss Marsha's Purple Prose Potion. She made it just for all y'all authors. It's honey-based, but it's not sticky, I promise. The Egyptians used honey for healing whatever ails ya." She paused only to rush on again. "Forgive my yammering. Now that I know you're my client, I'm plumb nervous as a bride on her weddin' night. I'll be back right quick." Then she blushed, giggled, and exited. The woman seemed as bubbly as Sunny Days had been.

Paige slipped out of her outfit, carefully and precisely folded her clothes perfectly, and placed them in the covered basket, replacing the wicker top. She climbed on the massage table, pulled the lavender-scented sheet over her naked body, and almost gave into her fatigue and jet lag.

A mellow melody that Paige could swear was the new age version of Prince's Purple Rain played from discreetly hidden speakers. She chuckled. *How apt for the rustic on the outside, purple on the inside palace.* Paige had a feeling Sunny had played a large part in designing the Spa Haus and developing the ambience of the place.

In minutes, Tully reappeared. "Normally, I'm not this scatterbrained motor mouth" — then she laughed — "Who am I kiddin'? I'll shut up now and let my fingers do the talking." She worked quietly for a second, two at the most. "My, but you are wound tighter than a string on a fiddle." When she started working the upper chest, Paige winced.

"You are tighter than most. You under stress?"

Paige just groaned in response.

Tully's word salad ceased as her skillful hands worked the knots out of Paige's muscles. Not long after Tully told her to *roll on yer tummy*, Paige started to drift off.

Tully excused herself for a moment, saying she was going to switch things up with some new eucalyptus lotion they just received. A cool breeze stirred the air as she exited the room.

Paige welcomed the coolness after suffering the heat of the day. Her body remained relaxed, with her face buried in the donut at the head of the table.

Suddenly, she felt something wet on her toes and swore she could hear a scramble and a series of clicks on the vinyl floor. She briefly wondered if Tully was wiping her feet with a damp towel, but that was crazy since the woman left the room. Plus, it didn't account for the sounds of shuffling she sensed near her.

She raised her head, glanced over her shoulder, and saw a large black shadow and four smaller ones. *Holy Shit!* Her brain struggled to process the scene. Her breath froze in her lungs. *That's no shadow.* A big black bear and her cubs were at the foot of the bed. With her. In this room. Was that a bear cub nuzzling her toes?

CHAPTER SEVEN: A BEARY CLOSE ENCOUNTER

Booker paused, enjoying the moonlight and nature at its finest. He inhaled a deep breath of pure mountain air, taking in the cedar and hickory scent of the forest. As he moseyed along the pathway, a naked woman suddenly burst out of the Spa Haus, followed by a mother bear and four cubs in wobbly pursuit. He froze in place, staring, not believing his eyes when he recognized the woman.

Paige screamed, "Don't just stand there. Do something, anything!"

"Unholy hell!" He grabbed the mallet next to the huge ornamental gong and whacked the hell out of it. The sound reverberated louder than anything he had heard so far in those parts.

Paige stopped and covered her ears, and the bears veered away from the noise. A cacophony of hisses, grunts, barking, and yelling filled the air, and then all hell broke loose. Tiny tore after the five bears while Sunny, Jesse, and another young man rushed there from all directions, shouting and pelting the bears with rocks they picked up.

The mother bear rose on her hind legs and roared. The cubs shot straight up, sniffing hard, perhaps to assess what their mother sensed. Then they woozily started to wobble away. Another growl from mama bear made certain the cubs followed, and they finally melted into the wilderness as if nothing had happened. It was almost comical.

Booker bent at the waist, out of breath, huffing and puffing as if he had been running. But Paige and the others were the ones who'd done that. His gaze found Paige, who looked down at herself, and if possible, got even whiter when she appeared to realize she was buck-naked. She collapsed to the ground and unwound the small towel holding her hair, apparently attempting — but failing — to cover herself.

Booker appreciated her efforts, but he had already caught the curve of her hips, the flash of long legs, thighs, and full breasts. He wisely restrained his wolf whistle and ignored the stirring of his groin, because Paige looked like she could spit silver bullets. Another woman, hysterical with nervous laughter, ran to Paige and threw a sheet over her shoulders.

Paige fashioned the sheet into a toga, draping it on her mighty fine body. "Thanks, Tully."

Booker loved how Paige's wild blonde hair framed her beautiful face. She looked like she just got out of bed.

"Tarnation!" someone shouted.

Booker turned to see Jesse walking to the spa door.

"That mama bear figured out how to undo the latch. This door needs a bear-proof lock. That mama just taught her cubs how to undo latches." Jesse peered at the lock and set about remedying the situation with a laugh.

Paige's voice shook when she said, "I need a stiff drink."

"So do I," Booker added.

Jesse angled his head inside the door. "Sunny keeps some moonshine inside the spa."

Sunny stood behind a counter, pouring a clear liquid from a jug. She saved the day by offering Mason jars of moonshine to all those who came to the rescue.

Paige hesitated. "I'm afraid to drink in here with no lock on the door after what happened!"

Jesse joined them at the counter. "I got the lock rigged so she can't open it again. It's bear-proofed now. You can relax."

He picked up a jar and handed it to her.

Paige took it with shaky hands and smiled gratefully. "Thanks, Jesse. Don't mind if I do."

Tully grabbed one of the Mason jars, now recovered from her hysterical laughter. "No worries 'bout them bears. Both the honey lotion and the soap bars those imps took off with contain cannabis. They're all likely higher than kites by now, so that bear squad won't be botherin' us anymore tonight, at least. I suggest, Miss Paige, you take a soak in our mineral pool. I think y'all may prefer that instead of a massage."

Paige agreed. "Good idea. I packed a bathing suit but left it in my cabin."

"Mind if I join you?" Booker asked, briefly glancing down her body. "Your birthday suit would be perfect and easier to get into. You know . . . to soak away that honey residue."

She gave him a saucy wink. "Sounds like you've had a honey massage here, too."

"No, but I believe my fast thinking earned me the right to a nice hot soak, too. After all, I did wrangle with five bears." He held up his hand, wiggling his fingers. "Count them — five. Surely my heroic action to summon the cavalry and rescue the fair maiden is reward-worthy. Doesn't that make me your hero?"

Paige fluttered her lashes and raised her palm to cover her heart. "Yes."

Booker's rod stirred behind his zipper.

Then Paige winked. "Kinda, but only if it was written in my romance novels. This is real life." She waltzed up to him, gave him a sweet kiss packed with heat, then sauntered toward an inner door.

His groin twitched again as he rushed to open the door for her. "After you, fair maid." As she passed through, he muttered, "You are not supposed to run from bears, you know. They'll think you're prey."

"Yeah, I know. I read the pamphlet in my cabin." Paige frowned. "Besides, I didn't run at first. I pitched some honey-scented soap bars in their direction and backed out of the room slowly—very slowly." She used a drawn-out, sexy tone when she said *slowly*. "Once outside the room, I ran as fast as I could while they were distracted. It wasn't until everything calmed down that I noticed I was naked."

Booker grinned. "So I noticed."

They entered the room with the pool, and Paige boldly shed her toga and smoothly lowered herself into the scented mineral-laced water.

Booker nearly swallowed his tongue but quickly disrobed and followed her into the pool.

Paige leaned close to him and purred, "My hero." She traced his lips oh-so-lightly with the tip of her tongue.

Booker responded by deepening the kiss, drawing her against him, and wrapping an arm around her waist. She quivered, sending tingling sensations down his spine to settle in his groin. She burrowed closer, and his head filled with her scent mixed with the fragrance of the mineral water and what had to be the aroma of cannabis from incense burning somewhere. The combination was intoxicating.

Eureka! I'm following my script as if I'm the leading character in my novel. If I wrote this scene, I'd spice things up right about now. Paige nearly lost herself in Booker's intoxicating kiss. However, her inner Freud interrupted when her id went into overdrive. *This can't happen. Not here. Not yet.*

Her rational brain knew she had to break this up. Her author's brain wanted to let her passion loose. Let her desires have free reign. Let the tension mount. Let it build. Let it burn. Let it flame. The problem with that battle here and now was that it was great for fiction, devastating for reality. What complicated things further was that her inner author was winning the war because she didn't want to just kindle the fire and let it burn naturally. Instead, she yearned to pour gasoline on the whole thing.

She wanted his penis to impale her and let her heat swallow every last inch of him. She wanted to tear at his body, kiss the spots where she left scratches, dig her fingers into his full head of hair, lick his penis until it wept, and have her way with him completely and totally.

With an intense effort, she kissed him less intensely and slid out of his arms. "Whoa, Nelly. I'm letting myself get carried away."

"It was fine with me." He looked down at his rod. "I'm up for it."

"So I see." She giggled. "Do you have a marsupial pouch on you?"

He frowned. "I'm not following."

She peered at his abdomen. "I don't see one." She probed his belly with her fingertips. "Nope. Don't feel one either."

"Careful, you're playing with fire again." He stopped her hand. "What are you looking for?"

"A condom. Safe sex."

He raised his brow. "Not to be indelicate, but you're not likely to get pregnant, are you?"

"Two things. First, I'll answer your question. No. Not likely. I'm post-menopausal."

His face clouded with confusion. "Interesting. What could thing two be?"

"STDs and privacy. Someone has to lock up tonight, and we don't need to create a scandal, thus upsetting our fans."

He nodded, and she knew he understood when she noticed more than his face deflating as he shifted away from her.

"Let's play football," she suggested.

He squinted at her. "Huh?"

"Consider this an intercepted pass."

"Feels like a time out."

She nodded. "But the clock is still running."

He grinned. "I see, so it's not over."

She smiled. "It's a delay with a re-match scheduled soon."

"Good enough."

Paige peered at him. "I'm not ready to call the game, though. I'd like some time on the clock for a huddle."

He visibly relaxed and changed the subject. "You have a keynote address tomorrow, don't you?"

"I do."

"Whatcha gonna talk about?"

She sent him a playful glance. "Writing."

He splashed her. "No kidding?"

She splashed back. "Things that work, things that don't."

He smiled. "Are you going to tell them the standard *write what you know*?"

"That, of course, and more."

"Pray tell. Or are you gonna cop out and say *wait and see*?"

"Never."

He prodded further. "Out with it, then."

She cleared her throat and sank lower into the water. Without his body heat, she was growing cold. "Sunny Days is the Master or Mistress of Ceremonies, so after she gets the housekeeping details cleaned up and introduces me, I plan to open with . . . Writing for sales is easy. Simply cut open a vein."

He grinned and chuckled. "I like that."

She smiled, nodding. "Writing's not for sissies. Gotta take rejection. Cut your words till they cry."

He agreed, adding, "Or you will cry if you don't. Sounds like you're in good shape." His gaze traveled slowly down her body. "In every way."

She blushed and sank lower into the cooling pool. "Then I'll launch into my Seven Steps to Writing Success."

"Please share . . ."

"Believe me. I will." She grinned, stepping out of the water and wrapping the sheet around her. "Tomorrow."

He slapped the water. "I hear what you did there." Then he gave her a wolf whistle as she headed for the door.

"Hold on." He caught up to her, pulled her close, and gave her a tender kiss.

She looked at him, confused.

"A kiss . . ." he murmured.

She tilted her head.

"For luck."

She smiled sweetly, trying to restrain the heat his kiss ignited.

Chapter Eight: A Match

What have I done? Sunny Days shook her head. *I wish I didn't have so* much *to do.* Sunny smiled as she thought of her baby, Windy, relieved that her twin, Storme, was watching her toddler as she spent the day juggling her many tasks.

While she was excited to be the host for the NWASDS, it was a lot of work. As the Soirée Conference Chairperson, the role came with more tasks than she had anticipated. Mercifully, the company the conference board had hired to oversee registration had been doing a stellar job—so far. At least no problems had reached her desk.

Sunny pulled up her punch list and reviewed it. Many things could be checked off now, thank heaven. However, one particular task overlapped her conference responsibilities and her side job as a matchmaker. *Hmm . . . I just may have the perfect solution to kill two birds with one stone.*

She smiled, imagining the conversation with Storme if her twin were to learn what she planned to do.

"Can't do that," Storme would say.

"Can too," I would reply.

"Cannot."

"Watch me."

Sunny grinned as she made the switch to the ATC registrants list. Then she pressed *Print* on her keyboard. The deed was done with no one the wiser. It was almost too easy. *With one keystroke – okay, two keystrokes – I successfully put Operation Paige-Turner into action, completing both my matchmaking job and my conference work. Sometimes, things fall right smack into place. By adding Booker Turner and myself to Paige Newhart's Writers Triad, I can moderate the duo and cash in on my hunch. Those two have some serious sparks flying between them.* Through their writing triad, she knew she could nudge those sparks into a nice fire. In addition, she could also learn a lot from them for her writing career. It was a win-win.

Sunny had experienced a deep gut feeling when she first saw Paige and recalled that Paige had registered for a match-making appointment. *I found a way to make it happen. I put her in range for Cupid's arrow. A few more encounters similar to last night's at the Spa Haus, and it's a fait accompli.* Sunny buffed her nails on her chest, congratulating herself. *Cinderella is in place. It's time for Operation Cinderfella to begin.*

Sunny sat back and re-checked her punch list. She pulled up the document for her opening remarks, added a few housekeeping notes, and then checked the agenda for the day.

Keynote Address, Paige Newhart
Break Out Sessions
Lunch
Writers Triad Challenge
Dinner
After Word with Storme Knight

Chapter Nine: Talk about Love

Paige reviewed her notes for her keynote speech, which she titled *Seven Simple Steps to Stellar Success*. She would begin with an icebreaker exercise to warm up her audience, giving them five minutes to share scenes from their latest stories with the people next to them.

She reviewed the rest of the speech, which focused her talk on what she coined her *Seven Ss* — Seven Simple Secret Scandalous Steps to Stellar Success. She laughed, pleased with herself. *If Donna Karan can build a wardrobe with seven easy pieces of clothing, then I can create a keynote address using a similar system. It's easy to base the approach on how I usually start my writing process. Start with a siren and a secret, then along comes a seduction and a scandal, a follow-up shitstorm, and a spicy, satisfying conclusion. Viola! Paige Newhart's Seven Simple Steps to Success.* In her notes, she'd added a joke about seasoning all that with sensational sex, the all-important secret sauce of writing romance. Throughout her talk, she inserted tried and truisms she had gathered throughout her career.

One specific source came to mind as she added the topics Booker had mentioned in the hot mineral waters the previous night. *Mmm . . . last night, when his taut chest hairs tickled my tits, and his rod danced and threatened to penetrate. When his kisses and the feel of his muscles made me scratch and scream and had me panting with want and roaring with need. Last night, when I wanted him to impale me. Ahh, how sweet it was . . .*

She glanced at the clock and realized she didn't have time for such torrid thoughts. She had a keynote to deliver. It was time to dress. She decided to wear the charcoal Kentucky Derby-worthy column sheath dress with cape-draped sleeves, a classic yet elegant creation. She sat and slid her feet into black pumps, going for sheer chic. She had seen Alex and Tiny earlier, and Alex said he would drive her to the convention center soon, so she gathered her things and applied her lipstick.

Sunny sped through their mountain ridge home at warp speed, grabbing her tablet and wristlet clutch. She quickly bussed Windy's head as her toddler tottered off to join her cousin, Misty Knight.

The girls wobbled off, tugging Holly's tail while her crafty child called, "Bye-bye."

Sunny tried to brush Jesse's lips the same way, but he pulled her into a deeper kiss.

"Later," he murmured with a gleam in his eye that still showed his love even after several years of marriage and new parenthood.

"Break a leg and all that," her twin Storme called.

On the fly, Sunny answered, "No one says that to the Masters of Ceremonies, ya know."

"Do too."

"Do not."

Jesse intervened. "I hate to break off this sister talk thingy, but you're going to be late, Sunny."

Sunny jerked to attention. "Right. I'll be back. After the keynote and once I know Gatlinburg by Night is launched," she cautioned.

"Don't hold your breath, Jess," Storme warned. "I can send Craig over if you need backup childcare."

Jesse puffed out his chest. "I can deal."

Sunny hopped into her sensible sedan, which she referred

to as the *mom mobile*, and headed to town.

The attendees could travel, register, and then take in the sights, walk the strip, or simply collapse for the night. Instead of the typical conference early morning format, this Great Smoky Mountain Soirée promised the attendees plenty of time to relax, recuperate, and rejuvenate in the lush green beauty of the surrounding mountains and national park.

This day's agenda included a late morning hot breakfast earlier, leaving the afternoon free so attendees could take in the attractions and sightseeing in the city or browse the Vendor's Exhibits before meeting up again to sip a cocktail during social hour and enjoy the opening night banquet in the Tennessee Ballroom. Now everyone was heading to the Greenbrier Auditorium with its southern comfort theater seats to hear Paige A. Newhart's Seven Simple Steps to Stellar Success Keynote Address.

As the conference host, Sunny already knew that Paige's speech would include all things bling, glitz, and glamour. *What fun!* Sunny and Storme had collaborated to fill the Conference Swag Bags with all sorts of bling. Storme had also commissioned their mother to donate purple velvet sleep masks trimmed with silver sequins that, of course, contained cannabis to promote pleasant sleep.

Sunny breezed through the venue on her way to the auditorium, happy to see everything was going smoothly. She mentally recalled the few details she wanted to mention during her introduction. She paused at the foot of the stage, took a swig from her bottle of water, ran her fingers through her curls, and then mounted the steps to the podium.

After checking the mic, she announced, "Howdy, y'all, welcome to the National Writers Association Southern Division Soirée. I'm Sunny Days, Conference Chairwoman." She spent a few minutes explaining some of the week's agendas, which would be taking place in the afternoons or evenings. It was a soirée, after all. "I hope y'all enjoyed your first day of the conference so far. We are extending our southern hospitality by opening with an *evening* kick-off to switch things up, hopefully making this conference unforgettable for y'all. Our keynote speaker tonight needs no introduction, as I'm sure most of you know the Queen of all things Romance. I'm pleased to present the one . . . the only . . . Paige A. Newhart. Take it away, Paige."

Paige approached the podium, waving at the audience like the romance royalty she was, and waited for the thunderous applause to simmer down before she began. "I'm delighted to be here. Thank you for that warm southern welcome. I'm going to kick this off with an icebreaker. Who knows? You might make a new friend and perhaps find another beta reader. Now, turn to someone near you and introduce yourself, then share a scene from one of your recent books. You might even exchange contact info for future reference."

Fortunately, the audience jumped into the icebreaker with enthusiasm, giving Paige a chance to gather her energy, take one last look at her notes, and prepare to deliver for the crowd.

After five minutes—give or take—passed, she whistled and laughed, drawing the audience's attention. "Did everyone find a new friend? Anyone get a new beta reader?" She looked at the sea of faces and saw several hands go up, some clasped and raised together.

"Yes? Excellent. Now, settle down, and I'll begin with a little reminder. Writing is easy . . ."

The crowd reacted, chattering, protesting, shaking heads, and laughing.

She glared at them and held up a hand. "Hear me out." She nodded, then smiled. "Writing is easy. Just get a knife and cut open a vein."

The crowd roared in response.

"You think that's something? Wait until your editors suggest cutting your baby. I swear, as your manuscript bleeds, so do you. After all, your writing is your heart and soul splashed onto the page. Am I right?" Paige waited a minute for the applause to quiet. "Over the years, I've honed my craft and finally uncovered the secret to success. There are seven simple steps. What I like to call my seven Ss." She raised her fingers and began to tick off each step. "All you need is a siren, a secret, a seduction, a scandal, a shitstorm, a dash of spice, and a satisfying conclusion. Is that all, you ask?" She raised her hand to her ear as if to hear them ask. "Au contraire . . . You need to add the secret sauce of writing . . . sensational sex. It's that simple." She paused, hearing a few grumbles, then whispered into the mic, "Shh, everyone, sex sells. Let me elaborate."

Paige went through each point with amusing anecdotes and examples from her books. As she neared the end of her talk, she added the tried-and-true things every writer ever heard. "Throw out your first three chapters. Your story starts in chapter four." She went on. "Write what you know and know the deets about where your story's set. Readers will catch mistakes. Don't forget to read other authors and see how they do things. I hear other writers ask, *where do you get your ideas?* I get mine from life, from *my* life, ripped from the headlines or tabloids." She winked. "And then I just make shit up."

The audience laughed.

"Writing is one of the few jobs with a license to kill." She heard more laughter and continued. "Be sure to kill off the haters and evil exes in your stories, foil the plan to poison the protagonist, and use your words legally to annihilate the antagonist. Write that shit well." She shook her finger. "Study your craft." She left the podium, walked to center stage with the mic in hand, and bent forward. "Remember, no one can tell your story the way you can. Thank you all for your attention. I hope you enjoy the Night on Gatlinburg's After Word. My books are available at the Vendor's Exhibit. Check your program for the Book Signing schedules. Thank you, conference committee, for your southern hospitality. With the stroke of the pen, With the press of a key. It's all in your hands. Write on!" She bent in a graceful bow and left the stage, blowing kisses and handing the mic to Sunny.

The crowd gave her a vigorous send-off.

Sunny returned to the stage with more announcements. "That was amazing. Thank you, Paige Newhart. Before y'all head out to tour the town tonight, I have a few gentle reminders. For the early birds, there are round table discussions tomorrow morning beginning at eight in the Tennessee Room that will discuss a variety of topics. Check your program for specifics. Tomorrow, we'll launch our Writers Triad Challenge. The WTC links experienced authors with aspiring and debut authors to write a novelette that will be compiled into an anthology. The book will be available next year, and the proceeds will be used as a fundraiser for a worthy cause. Our Writer's Retreat, a month-long extension of this soirée to write and learn with other writers, is still open for enrollment. To join us, sign-up is available in the Author's Lair.

"The WTC teams are listed on the handouts at the exits, and they will take place on Level One in the Mills Room terrace—weather permitting. Workshops will be held concurrently in the Greenbriar, Tennessee, and Elkmont Rooms. Book signings will be held in the evening in Ballroom A. A schedule has been posted there. The exhibits and vendors will open after lunch tomorrow on the Lower Level. Be sure you take advantage of all these opportunities. I hope you enjoy your evening. Happy writing, everyone."

Paige exhaled. *The hard part's over. Now for the fun part.* Fans swarmed around her, snapshots and selfies were taken, everyone competing for her attention. She didn't see Booker. She looked past the flashing cameras, checking the crowd, but didn't see Booker anywhere. Apparently, he wasn't there. No big deal. They'd cross paths sooner or later. Was he letting her have her moment? Was he avoiding her? Or the flashing cameras? None of the above?

After the bustle died down, Paige made her way backstage, where she was scheduled for a post-talk Meet and Greet. There'd be a Wine and Dine later.

Her fans met her with a chorus of . . .

"Love your work."

"Can I get your autograph?"

"Great books!"

"I'm your biggest fan."

"No, I am," a curly moppet said.

"When's the next one coming out?"

Paige smiled. "You fans are the greatest. This never gets old." She signed several books quickly, happily accepting their comments. She was excited that everything went well. *Hmmm. Not that I'm looking for him, but where's Booker?*

CHAPTER TEN: FIND ME A MAN

Sunny Days noticed Booker slipping away. Oh, she knew where the man was headed. After all, she had taken several steps to ensure some matchmaker magic was afoot and on schedule. In roughly thirty minutes, Cupid's couple were set up to collide and find themselves in hot steamy water once again. She'd bet her firstborn, well maybe not her firstborn, but she'd bet money on it. She buffed her fingers on her chest. *I played a key role in this one.* She smiled. Oh yes, she was mighty proud of herself. She hummed the Matchmaker song from Fiddler on the Roof as she left the conference center.

Paige was happy to see Alex and Tiny at the exit door. Tiny was barking up a storm, and Alex was hanging out the car window hollering. *Good. Tiny's in his crate, so he can't knock me over.*

She got in the car, saying, "Nice wheels. Where'd you get them? And thank you for crating Tiny."

Amid Tiny's loud welcome, Alex grinned. "Storme Knight lent me Samson. Tiny can't do much damage in this vehicle."

Paige looked around. "Samson?"

"Storme apparently names everything and named this wreck *Samson*. This rattletrap of a vehicle is the perfect transport for your boy —"

"Tex's boy. My custody is temporary."

"Whatever. I suggest we get you back to the Lodge so you can take a walk with us. Tiny's been pining for you."

"Okey-Dokey." She nodded. "Home, James."

The traffic was heavy, with pedestrians crossing every which way, cruisers sailing along in their pick-ups and open-air Jeeps, and unsynchronized traffic lights holding things up. Slowly but surely, Alex was finally able to navigate through it all. Once they got past all the hubbub, they drove beneath the treetops into the National Park.

A thousand diamonds in the night sky pierced the tree canopy. The night was warmer than she expected. As the Lodge's gravel roadway crunched beneath Samson's wheels, she sighed in happy relief as they pulled up to her cabin. She rushed inside to exchange her designer clothes for comfortable leisure wear. Once she had, she met Alex and Tiny outside.

Tiny was beside himself, reconnecting with her. After vigorous petting, she ruffled his fur and managed to maneuver the beast through the woods. As they approached an unlit structure, Alex handed her a skeleton key.

"What's this?"

"The key to the Spa Haus. Sunny thought you'd like to soak off the stress of your day. You have the place to yourself. She reserved it for a private party."

She turned the key over in her hand. "Mmm. Wonderful. That sounds perfect. Wait ... I don't have a suit." She thought a moment. "And I don't want to crash anyone's party."

"You have an after-hours reservation for a *party* of one. You." He winked. "And you do have a suit."

"Huh?"

"Your birthday suit."

Paige laughed, handed the leash to Alex, and unlocked the back door of the Spa Haus, which led directly to the mineral pool. Low lights twinkled over the gently bubbling surface of the steamy mineral water. She shed her clothes and sighed as she slipped into the soothing heat.

From the shadows, she heard a low, sexy voice purr, "Fancy meeting you here." Booker grinned.

She was startled, to say the least, but managed to quip, "Right back atcha. Are you stalking me?"

"It's beginning to look that way, but I'm innocent. I made an after-hours reservation earlier today, and here I am." He removed his clothes and joined her in the pool.

Paige nearly swallowed her tongue, seeing his glorious naked body again. "And so you are. Sunny is a sly little wench, isn't she? She had Alex give me the key to the spa so I could relax in *private*." Through the rising steam, she sent a questioning glance. "I thought you'd be touring the town, painting it red, and partying with Storme's After Words excursion."

"Then you'd be wrong, wouldn't you?" He smiled. "Seriously, though, great talk. Loved the humor. And the advice was right on. Solid."

"I see. You liked the part about not frontloading the manuscript with the back story?"

"Yep. Weaving it throughout is the way to go." He moved close to her, wearing a wicked smile. "Whatever. I say we celebrate your successful keynote address and enjoy this time together. What do you say?"

She leaned into him and gave him a teasing kiss. "Whatever you say."

Booker wrapped his arms around her and deepened the kiss. His lips were hot, spicy, intoxicating, and more. Much, much more.

Her nipples tightened in response to his fingers brushing across her torso. She welcomed those intoxicating touches and all his other body parts pressing against her with open arms. She had a feeling that soon, very, very soon, her legs would follow suit.

She meshed her body with his, entwining him in her arms

71

and nearly melting in their combined heat. She enjoyed the tango of their tongues, the taste of him rich and deep like dark chocolate. She felt his kiss everywhere. In her heart. In her soul. In her core. Delicious shivers ran down her spine, driving her nuts with desire. Her pulse raced, and she raised her legs to wrap around his hips. He entered her without hesitation, his rod hot and hard.

When he started moving, she soared. Truth be told, she became dizzy as her body spasmed with her shattering release. She collapsed against his solid chest and played with the curls she found there. She drew in a series of shallow breaths, listening as their heartbeats began to sync.

After a long, satisfied sigh, she said, "Running into each other is becoming a habit. I like it."

"Good to hear," he returned. "Same here."

"Habits are hard to break," she warned.

"But healthy habits lead to good ones. And this"—he kissed her again—"is definitely a good one."

"I'm getting quite attached to you, and we can't have that," she said, detaching herself.

"Why not?"

"Because I'm married."

"What? Since when?" He paused, then chuckled. "Married to your work's okay with me."

She laughed. "So, I'm not cheating?"

"Nope. But this" —he wiggled his finger back and forth between them—"could seriously end your single status."

She laughed again, enjoying his blarney. "My work pays the bills."

He nodded. "It also kept you single and fortunately available for when I crossed your path."

"Hmm. So, it has."

"You know what I think?"

"No, pray tell. No doubt you will."

He winked. " Like aged wine, love's greater later."

She giggled. "I'll say this. Older's bolder. Kids don't have any idea how sweet it is when you know what you're doing." She slid out of his arms and out of the pool. "You have other Bear-y important things to do." She picked up a plush towel nearby and dried off.

"I do?" He thought for a second. And grinned. "Clever. Bear probably does need to go outside. It has been a while since I took her out."

Paige donned her clothes, watching as Booker ran a towel over his delectable body. She sighed when he covered it with clothing.

He walked her back to her cabin and left after a quick kiss, no doubt in a hurry to check on Bear after she'd been cooped up for so long. The slight nip in the night air made her shiver as she entered her cabin, glad she had Alex to care for Tiny.

She got ready for bed, washed her face, and then applied her favorite skin cream that contained hyaluronic acid and retinol. It was time to focus on herself if she was to accomplish her goal of finding her Mr. Right. *Maybe I already have. Booker's ticking all the boxes.*

Paige lay naked between cozy sheets covered with a Hudson blanket, remembering Booker's fresh clean scent that wafted in the mist created by the heated water. She felt herself reacting to the sensations she'd experienced as he learned her body. He had studied her like a foreign language, learning the words and places on her body that made her melt. She didn't need Google to tell her what she had learned of him. The memory of his steady heartbeat followed her into sweet but steamy dreams.

CHAPTER ELEVEN: ALL TOGETHER

Paige got up to a misty morning. The day felt perfect, neither hot nor cold. She didn't need a robe. Wisps of cloud glazed the apricot leaves visible through her window. Poofs of mist rested above several trees that displayed the colors of a summer fruit salad. Periodically a break in the haze revealed a pineapple-yellow leaf next to a mango-hued one. Another glimpse of apricot was on display, contrasting with the green of a honeydew melon. The brown of the stalk created and somehow united an awesome autumn view unlike any she'd ever seen. It gave her inspiration not only for her writing but also provided the outfit she'd wear that morning. She selected a long-sleeved taupe jumpsuit topped with the traditional autumn-colored fringed light wool poncho.

Before she did anything else, she typed reminder words into her notes on her cellphone.

Van Gogh of mountain color.

Tangerine leaves.

Autumn in the Smokies makes wordsmiths of mathematicians and poets out of scientists.

Summer salad of banana, watermelon, apricot, kiwi, plum, and lemon colors.

Not the stock of usual scarlets, mustard, orange, ruby reds, emeralds, browns, and golds.

Lemon-hued leaves lay like Christmas bulbs on the evergreen's branches.

Satisfied with her notes, she stopped. *What happened to my six a.m. to six p.m. writing process? I'd never slack off like this at home. Is this the mountain magic Sunny talks about, or is Booker jamming up my circuitry?* She wasn't sure but shrugged it off.

She grabbed her computer bag and crossbody purse and left her cabin to search for Alex and Tiny. It wasn't long before she found Tiny sniffing and pawing a log. When his doggy nose broke off a section of bark, he snorted and sneezed. *Good Lord, don't tell me the silly dog has allergies.* Tiny began gnawing the bark.

"Leave it," Alex commanded.

To Paige's amazement, Tiny dropped the bark and turned his attention to Paige's arrival with his typical enthusiastic greeting.

"Down, boy. I miss you, too." She ruffled Tiny's fur while struggling to remain standing.

Alex got Tiny under control and asked, "How ya doing, Paige? All set for the Meet and Greet this morning? Don't forget the WTC this afternoon, being held in the Mills Room. Offhand, I'm not sure if it will be on the terrace or inside." He turned his attention back to the excited dog. "Sit, Tiny."

Tiny sat.

"Do you know who I'm scheduled to write with?"

"I checked the list last night, and someone has a sense of humor. You're listed as the lead author, but the other two are listed as *mystery writers.*"

"Hmm. I sure hope they know who they are and where to go—"

"Not our problem. I'm sure the coordinator has it under control."

Paige nodded. "Guess I'll find out when I get there. No biggie. Are you driving me today?"

"Yup. I'm at your service. I plan to spend the day handling your correspondence, working from my cabin to keep an eye on Tiny. I'll wear him out first, so he'll nap while I take care of business. Text me if you need anything."

They walked Tiny back to Alex's Old Mother Hubbard

cabin. Alex crated Tiny, gave him a bone, then led Paige to the gravel parking lot.

Once they reached the vehicle called Samson, Alex opened the passenger door and bowed with a flourish to usher her inside. "Your chariot awaits, boss lady." Once Paige was settled and seat-belted properly, he said, "Parking in town is a pain. I'll drop you off at the Historic Nature Trail entrance."

Paige couldn't help but see what he was talking about as they hit downtown. "It seems like everyone and their brother is in town. Can't be the writer's conference that's got this place hopping."

Alex's eyes popped. "Look around you, boss lady. See those pumpkin people scattered here and there?"

"Huh?"

"It's fall. In the Smokies. Please note the color changes of the leaves, the gaping tourists, scarecrows, pumpkins, and cornstalks abounding and astounding the eye. You need to get out while you're here and take advantage of all this. Sunny went out of her way to build sessions around opportunities to write in the park or sightsee in the Great Smoky Mountain National Park. You might want to take your writing triad down to Mynatt Park. You've got your laptop, and picnic tables are set up next to a babbling creek. Took Tiny there, the place is gorgeous."

"Let me see how things go. I just might." She had to admit the prospect of seeing the color changes and taking advantage of the temperate days held appeal. No doubt it was much cooler back home in New York. *Occasionally, I must have glanced at Central Park during the fall.* But when she thought about it, no scene arose in her mind's eye. *Could I have worked through the color change at home and not even noticed?* Were there fairy lights? She didn't know for sure. But she did see that it was breathtaking here. The deep green and shade of the surrounding evergreens interspersed with golden trees glowing like a lamppost created a startling contrast and spectacular image.

"It's time to head for the hills, boss."

Paige smiled, since they were already in the hills. She looked around at the kaleidoscope of color. "I have to admit I've never seen such a variety of fall hues. The browns are the color of toast." Her stomach growled. "Good thing they have a Continental Breakfast set up. I'm starved."

"By the way," he said, "I've got you all set up for your book signing in the Ballroom —"

"A or B?"

"A, and you're welcome."

"You know I think you are the best, right?"

Alex grinned as he turned onto Airport Road — no mean feat with the traffic and tourists swarming the street — and dropped her off. Once she got inside, she fished through her purse for her lanyard and speaker's ribbon and headed for the Author's Lair.

She greeted authors and fans with smiles and hellos as she grabbed a small plate and nibbled on a slice of pecan coffee cake. She added some honeydew melon and cantaloupe to make up for the pastry, making a mental note to add those melon colors to her writing notes.

She touched base with some notables, exchanged air kisses, chit-chatted with her writer friends, and wandered over to Ballroom A to participate in the book signing. True to his word, Alex had everything set up. He even made sure there was cold water with lemon and ice in a tall glass waiting for her.

Her new display banners included various shades of purple, reminding her of the interior of the Spa Haus. She giggled. *Who says I don't appreciate color?* The banners looked fabulous, and her books were artfully displayed. The overall presentation looked professional, mixed with her signature glitz and glamor. Her swag even included silver and purple Mardi Gras bead necklaces.

She checked out the other tables but failed to find the silver fox named Booker anywhere. She did notice a double-sized table with every kind of banner, bulletin, and easel she'd ever seen anywhere set up for Molly Made. The Molly Made's signature gold question mark adorned all the paraphernalia. That signature question mark always appeared where an author's picture should be and was as famous as Molly Made's books. But as usual, a representative from the publishing house was on hand to hand out what she assumed were pre-signed books, but not the reclusive, infamous Molly herself.

Why the big mystery? But Paige knew, of course. It was part of the Molly Made brand. She glanced again at her table, seeing her own glitzy brand shining back at her. *Mine stacks up. It's competitive. No biggie. No worries.*

Paige moved behind her table and greeted the event hostess, thanking her for the Gatlinburg Writers Guild member assigned to assist her. Usually, Elyse took care of those functions or at least liaised with those who could. She figured Alex must have set this one up.

The young assistant's face flushed, clearly star-struck, and her voice came out in a rush. "Hello. I'm Amy. If there's anything you need, I'm here to help." Her hands flailed about. "I'll do anything you need. But before it gets crazy busy, would you autograph my copy?" In her haste to grab her copy, she knocked the easel aside, which sent a pile of business cards and books cascading over the table, about to land in a heap all over the floor.

Paige bent forward to prevent the books from falling at the same time as a set of arms stretched out to do the same. Her forehead knocked against the good Samaritan's with a loud clunk, sending her backward. Somewhat dazed, she flew her hand to her head as the books continued to slide. She scrambled to stop them and hit fumbling hands. "Whoops. So sorry." She looked up to see the hands belonged to Booker, who grinned as he sought to apologize and help Amy in the process.

Amy's face blazed red. "I'm such a klutz! I'm so sorry. Do either of you need ice?" She wrung her hands and went to snatch some ice from Paige's water glass, tipping it over and soaking everything nearby.

"Oh no!" Amy scrambled, looking around helplessly.

"Where's the *Bounty* when you need it?" Booker quipped, whipping out a handkerchief. He lifted a pile of books and dropped the handkerchief on the spill. Fortunately others around them, including some helpful fans, threw in tissues and napkins to help out.

Paige laughed, taking it all in stride. She stepped off to the side and began signing books while Amy helped to right things. Another guild member stepped in and helped with the sales transactions.

"I'd hoped to bump into you, but this"—he spread his arms wide—"I did not foresee."

He apparently noticed the water that had spilled on her breasts and suddenly grabbed a napkin from a fan and dabbed at the wet spot. His touch sent her heartbeat into overdrive.

She chuckled. "Thank heaven you showed up when you did."

"I see you're busy. Would you like to grab a bite when you're done here?" He smiled, revealing beautiful white teeth ringed by a charming yet wry smile.

Someone shoved a book at her. "Write *to my number one fan, Ann.*"

"Sure." Paige automatically took the book and autographed it as requested.

Booker took that moment to say, "Meet me across the street at the Arcadia Space Needle for lunch."

Startled, Paige looked up, slightly confused. *Space Needle?*

Arcade? Lunch? "Huh?"

From his pocket, Booker pulled a black pen with two bold silver M's scrawled lavishly across the surface. It held her attention for a brief second until he nabbed a swag notepad, wrote something, and slipped the note to Amy. "Please give her this when she's done."

Amy nodded.

Paige smiled and returned to her task, enjoying every moment of the steady stream of fans. *This is what it's all about. This never gets old.* With gratitude and smiles, she signed the morning away.

"I loved *Bedside Manor*," one fan enthused while picking up its companion, *Death Bed*. "It was a great way to continue Daphne and Dane's story, but I wouldn't want to be his next patient."

Paige laughed. "I'm glad you enjoyed it. Since his patients have an affinity for dying, I don't blame you one bit."

CHAPTER TWELVE: PINNACLE OF SUCCESS

Paige had talked herself out while signing books and was positively parched. She grabbed the bottle of water that Amy had miraculously produced at some point and took a sip. In the aftermath of the spill, Booker had seemed to melt away after helping Amy work on the clean-up. She'd wanted to thank him for his help, but the line of fans and book buyers didn't allow her time to speak with him. *I take advantage of every opportunity to hobnob with my fans for exposure. It helps sell books.*

Amy kept busy ringing up sales. She swiped her forehead and called out, "Paige, we're almost sold out!"

Just then, a gaggle of girls approached and bought the remainder of the books.

"Sold out!" Amy announced.

Paige smiled wide. She was tired, thirsty, and famished. She slumped briefly in her seat, then shook it off. The PA system played bell tones, indicating the book signing session was over. Paige stood and stretched. *The book signing went well, if I do say so myself.*

She turned to Amy and held out her hand. "It was nice working with you." She squeezed Amy's hand with appreciation.

Amy giggled. "If you say so. Sorry about the mess with the water."

"All's well that ends well." Paige turned to leave.

Amy moved to stop her. "Oh, I almost forgot. Wait." She scrambled through the swag and found a slip of paper. "Here ya go."

Paige turned toward her, befuddled. "Oh?"

Amy shoved the folded note at her. "That tall man fan, the one who helped mop things up, asked me to give this to you."

Thanking Amy, Paige unfolded the paper and read it. The bold handwriting somehow looked familiar. *Meet me for a meal to remember at* Slice Pizza Bakery *xo, Booker.* "Hold on a minute, Amy. Do you know a place called *Slice Pizza Bakery*?"

"Yes. It's a pizza place across the street. Just enter the Arcadia —"

"Arcade? Strange place for a pizzeria." She looked down at the note in her hand. Something about the scrawled words niggled at her, but she couldn't place it. *Where have I seen this handwriting?*

Amy shrugged. "It's a tourist town. People get hungry, and like a bowling alley, the convenience of easy-to-get food brings in beaucoup bucks."

"You're right. Thanks for pointing out the way. I'm off." She retrieved her purse and left the ballroom.

Paige stepped out into a gorgeous fall day with a beautiful October blue sky that highlighted the cherry red leaves of the maple tree growing beside the convention center near a huge grey boulder. On impulse, she aimed her cell phone at it and took a photo. She posted it, musing about a Van Gogh quote. Something about not having enough hands, enough canvases, and enough colors to paint the beauty of the fall season. *For me, it's not all that.* It's *about enough words.*

She used the crosswalk, but even so, she paused because the milling crowds were at odds with the traffic light. The intersection swelled with people. She couldn't imagine how she'd find Booker amid swarming crowds. Casting her trepidation aside, she entered the neon-lit building with the huge sign that read *Arcadia Space Needle*.

Once inside, Paige found the pizzeria and spotted Booker

right away. It wasn't such a challenge after all her worrying. His height, his nicely filled-out Nantucket Red pants worn with a startling white stand-up collar shirt—unbuttoned a tad, of course—and his GQ look made him stand out.

She joined him. "You're not signing books today? You disappeared after my waterworks."

He grinned. "No, this conference is for R and R. My attempt to combat burnout. My candle has been burning low."

She batted her eyes at him. "Oh no, can't have that. I may have a cure. Might put some pep in your step."

He winked. "Be my guest."

Paige glanced at the huge slices of pizza Booker had in his hands. The large size brought to mind the loud and proud MM she had seen on the pen Booker used to write his note. Come to think of it, Booker's handwriting resembled that monogram. *Where have I seen that before?*

Booker led her to a high-top seating duo where he rested the food. "Hope you don't mind. I ordered two slices. One with pepperoni and one with cheese. Which do you prefer?"

"Cheese, please."

Booker took the beverages from their recyclable container. "Sweet tea? Unsweetened?"

"Sweet tea sounds very southern, and being from the north, I'll give it a try." She took a sip. "Whoa, it is sweet all right." She folded the pizza slice in half—New York style—fumbling to catch the stringy melted cheese, laughing as she did, and dug in. "Mmm, good."

Booker smiled, agreeing. "I'll say. I'd give these four stars on size alone. Lucky for us, it tastes as good as it looks."

Booker glanced around and gestured to a ticket counter. "After this meal to remember, how about we board the Space Needle elevator and take a gander up top? A real bird's eye view. You up for it?"

"You wanna go up a Space *Needle?* Are *you* up for it, Mister

I'm afraid of needles? Are you sure about that?"

"To the top!"

Paige expected a long wait, judging from the crowds she'd seen so far, but there was next to no line for The Space Needle. Apparently, the pings and the dings of the arcade games distracted both the parents and their children, keeping them entertained. She had to admit, the din was festive, energetic, and electric. Even she got excited. *Is it the energy of the kids and games? Or Booker?*

Booker bought the tickets, and Paige preceded him into the unique glass elevator. They were the only two inside as they started the ascent. Booker took that moment to pull her close and snatch a lightning-quick kiss that sent electricity surging through her blood. He looked at her solicitously. "Are you afraid of heights?"

"Well, let's see." She pretended to be thinking. "You've taken me to some dazzlingly high places."

He tweaked her nose and hugged her closer to his side.

She laughed. "I'm not afraid of you." She winked. "Or what you do."

In less than ten minutes, they were surrounded by a white railing, standing on the observation deck. The panoramic view of the city and the mountains left her breathless. *Yeah. It's the view, you silly goose. Not his arms wrapped around me or his electric kiss.* Her attention was divided between competing views. *Hmm? Where to look first? The spectacular mountain splendor? The rustic mountain shops of Gatlinburg? The Lilliputian-sized tourists? Or the magnificent man standing beside me?*

She took in everything with a hand over her pounding heart. "Wow! This is spectacular. I didn't know I was looking for this all my life. This vista, this view, and how it makes me feel." she said, expelling a breath.

Booker responded with a tease. "You mean it's not me you were looking for?" He smiled and reached down to hold her hand. "It's nice to have someone share it with."

She squeezed his hand. "Can't say I have anyone special to share anything with."

"Oh? No special someone you haven't told me about yet?"

She shrugged. "No. Not really. I was too busy for anyone. How about you? Any significant other? A heartthrob tucked away? Someone *you've* kept secret?"

"Well, let's say I've sometimes been smitten but never bitten."

"Hmm. Are you up for a bite anytime soon?"

"You betcha."

She leaned into him and gave him what she hoped was a soul-searing kiss. The arrival of the next elevator brought a surge of tourists that pressed her body closer to his. Her body shuddered when she felt his hardness stirring, heating her blood and threatening to overload her circuits. She giggled.

"Sorry-not-sorry about the dance in my pants." He moved her out of the press of the crowd. "I blame you for the reaction."

She pressed into him again, enjoying the *rise* she got out of him.

He stepped away, grinned, cleared his throat, then turned and pointed to the telescopes conveniently and strategically placed around the observation deck. Signs next to each telescope spelled out what they would see through the lens. They checked out the manmade sights like Anakeesta, an adventure park, and the Skywalk, a suspension bridge stretched across two peaks and a valley. They also viewed the thrust of Mt. Le Conte and the Chimney Tops within the National Park.

Paige spotted some white trees that stood out, poking the sky like toothpicks that contrasted with the deep blue sky. "Wonder why that tree strand is so bare? The trees look like skeleton fingers or plastic knives slicing through the terrain. So stark." She shivered.

Booker's arm went around her, drawing her into his body

heat. With a heavy sigh, he read the sign next to the telescope out loud. *"The Chimney Tops Two Wildfire in twenty-sixteen killed fourteen people and two black bears, and burned over two-thousand-five hundred structures and approximately seventeen-thousand acres."*

She shuttered. "Oh no, that's terrible."

"Yeah."

A nearby child interrupted her thoughts, sounding on the verge of tears. "Mom, two of my friends and their mother died in that fire."

His mother patted his shoulder. "I remember, son. So sad," she murmured, pulling her child into a hug.

Paige took a deep breath of fresh mountain air. "Life is short. Better live it to the fullest." She shook it off and looked around, refocusing her attention on living life.

Far below, a large orange African safari-type vehicle caught her eye. "Hey, see that? Looks interesting. Wonder what that's all about?"

His gaze followed her pointed finger. "Must be some sort of tour or adventure ride. Wanna find out and try it?"

"Sure. Sounds like fun. Alex was riding me about not getting out in the mountains enough, so why not?"

"Alex? I thought there was no one—"

"He's my personal assistant."

"Well, I suppose we better do something about him *riding* you. We don't want that."

Paige wondered if Booker planned to ride her anytime soon. Like right now . . . to catch some afternoon delight? But no, can't have that, not here where there were too many people around anyway.

The shade formed by the angle of the sun and the air cooling made her aware of the lateness of the day. "Yikes, I've got an appointment. Gotta run. This has been nice." She gave him a quick kiss and caught the elevator down.

It appeared that he meant to follow her, but a family

blocked him before he could get on the elevator. "Catch you later," he called.

She waggled her fingers as the doors closed. "Later, gator."

Fortunately, the traffic light made crossing back to the convention center easier. Paige quickly grabbed the bag she'd stashed in the Author's Lair and headed to the Mills section, where a sign directed her to the Mills Terrace for the WTC writer's event.

The park-like terrace looked magical, a place where fairies might play, and certainly fueled the imagination. Huge rocks bordered the space. Strategically placed wrought iron tables, chairs, and benches provided a workable place amid the garden-like area. Paige headed for the table displaying her pre-assigned number.

Enough sunlight filtered through the trees to keep the temperature comfortable. A pit fire glowed in the center of the area against the waning afternoon sun. She knew she was there as the experienced author mentor and wondered who her partners would be. Her laptop was charged and ready to use. She had her lucky pen, her writer's notebook, her phone notes.

A few minutes later, Sunny Days popped in.

Paige set her writing gear down. "Hey there, Sunny. Great conference. Are you the moderator or just checking in for a hello?"

"I'm here in both capacities." Sunny's gaze held a glint of . . . something.

Paige grinned, suspecting some mischief from the gal. "How so?"

"I'm here to kick off the WTC, but as I told you, I'm a writer, too."

Paige nodded. "Yeah, I read some of your work in the brochures in my cabin. You've written a lot of the informational and promotional material for Sugarlands Lodge."

"Yes, but I've also written fiction under my Kathy Kalmar pen name." She broke off with a giggle. "I wrote a series beginning with *Beyond the Beach.*"

"Seriously?"

"No." Sunny winked and smiled again. "I lied. I write under Noreen Deplume." Her black mop top of curls bobbed as she shrugged. "Truth be told. *Beyond the Beach* belongs to the real Kathy Kalmar. I did write *Torrid in Toledo*, though. My story didn't have any spectacular scenery to speak of, but I made up for it with heat."

Paige raised a brow, surprised at Sunny's revelation. "I read that! You entered a writing contest I was judging. If my memory serves, you named the heroine Torrie, who carried a torch for Troy. Nice little chick-lit piece."

Sunny grinned. "I like alliteration."

Paige snapped her fingers. "That's why I remember it. Nice to have you aboard."

Sunny set her pens, pencil, and notepad on the table, then pulled a huge pink crystal from her tote bag.

Paige's curiosity got the better of her. "What's that for?"

"Oh, the crystal? It's part of my writing process. This crystal releases inspiration." She lifted out a smaller set of clear citrines. "These are for clarity." Then she lifted a purple spray bottle and spritzed lavender over the crystals. "This is my arsenal for aromatic therapeutic relaxation." Lastly, she pulled out a rosary and grinned. "So I don't let things get out of hand with my heat level."

Paige paused. "I'm impressed. How did you discover" — she waved her hand over Sunny's collection—"all this?"

"I'm the daughter of a hippie—"

"You don't say?"

"Turned entrepreneur."

Once again, Paige raised her brow in an unspoken

question.

Sunny winked. "My mom owns Mellow Magic Apothecary."

Paige felt as if her brows might become part of her upper forehead. "Quite a leap from free love, rock n roll, and pot. Oh wait . . . Mellow Magic supplies the pot-laced lotions at the Spa Haus, right?"

Sunny's grin widened, and she winked again. "Note the pot in *apot*hecary." She chuckled. "Mom also donated all the purple products you found in your conference Swag Bag. By the way, now you know my writing process, what's yours?"

Paige frowned. "I plot, outline, develop characters, and double-check my notes. Let's see . . . Other than comfy PJs, bunny slippers, a room with a view, and no clock, I'm all set to write here. I typically write from dawn to dusk. I'm not sure if that's a process, though, but it's how I roll. Once I know what I'm going to write, I write it."

"Whoa. With no clock, how do you know when to stop?"

"I get hungry. Ravenous, actually. Either that or my assistant interrupts me with food."

A deep male voice filtered through the noise of the other groups on the terrace in a smooth tone that sounded like velvet. Paige looked toward the sound to see Booker approaching her table.

He set two dice and a small tape recorder on the table. "Well, I'll be damned. Don't tell me you two are my writing buds."

Paige winced, quite surprised, certain her cheeks were flaming. She knew she could handle the addition of Sunny, but Booker, too? *Holy cow. I have my hands full with these two.* She cast a sharp look at Sunny and tilted her head toward Booker.

Sunny, who looked not quite innocent of any matchmaking shenanigans, glanced at her. "What?"

Paige raised her brow even higher.

Sunny just looked at her and shrugged. "I need to kick off this event. I'll be right back."

Paige returned the look and sighed heavily, on the verge of exasperation.

Sunny stood behind the podium and gained everyone's attention. "Good afternoon, everyone, and welcome to the Writers Triad Challenge. The object of this challenge is to team up experienced authors with aspiring and debut authors to write a ten-thousand-word romance novelette." She paused and glanced around the tables. "From the entries I received, I believe almost everyone participating here is a romance writer in some form or other. And don't forget, these stories will be compiled into an anthology to be used as a fundraiser for a worthy cause. You'll also need to come up with a nom de plume since you are writing as a triad. Have fun with that— my all-time fav was Ginger Ale. Write well, everyone."

Paige glanced at Booker but couldn't picture him as a romance writer.

Booker looked somewhat bemused but shook his head and shrugged. "Whatever."

Paige started things off after Sunny returned to the table. "I'm here as the mentor to beta read, critique, and assist but not necessarily write—unless asked, of course."

"I don't know much about the genre you are proposing, Sunny, but I'm game to explore whatever it is you want to do," Booker said. "I've been thinking of branching out. This is a great opportunity to do that."

Paige chuckled. "It will be interesting and fun to have a male perspective."

Booker shot her a questioning look but continued. "When I write, I ask myself *what if.* What about those who think a man can't write a convincing romance? What if we play with that concept? How about we write a male character writing as a woman? Or try this one. A female masquerading as a male author like Mary Ann Evans, aka George Elliot, who wrote *Silas Marner*?"

Paige simply shook her head. "Eh. Men write romances. No need to be sexist about it."

"But I'm not sure the reader would buy it. That a male could successfully pull off writing as a woman. *I* know men can, but do the readers?"

Paige frowned. "Why? Because his manliness would bleed through his writing? That's BS."

"Maybe. His writing might not be credible. Just saying we need to be careful," Booker warned.

"No need to over-complicate matters, Booker."

"Just saying. Things can get complicated fast."

Sunny broke up the exchange. "People, let's get back to writing. Booker, tell me about the *what-if* thingy. It sounds like an exciting way to begin. Give me an example."

Booker pressed the record key on his recorder, leaned back in his seat, and put his arms up behind his head. He crossed his legs, one over the other, and casually, almost in a dream tone, spoke. "What if there were two writers who plot a once-in-a-thousand-year storm, rising seas, a national park, politicians, scientists, and a family beach compound collide? At the same time, a rogue government ignites a worldwide war, and the war correspondent is female writing as a male?"

Sunny bounced in her seat. "What a novel idea! And add that the hot scientist clashes with an ultra-conservative politician whose part of environmental activists—"

Booker sat straight up. "What the hell? Why environmentalist? What does that have to do with this plot?"

Sunny pounced. "Where there's the sea, beach, and politicians, there's always environmentalists."

"Methinks this is too much material for a novelette," Paige interjected. "That's a real stretch for this genre. To your point,

Sunny, there's always an idealistic young gorgeous heroine tucked somewhere, because sex sells."

Paige could see both writers seemed to feed off each other, and despite her objections, a plot was emerging. "As a senior writer, I recommend you start plotting the setting—"

Sunny jumped in. "Whoa, Paige, I'm a pantser. I write as I go."

"Yes, but you must admit you have to start with a who and a where. Correct?"

Sunny nodded.

Booker broke in. "I propose we set the tale on Cape Cod."

"Why?" Sunny asked.

Booker ticked off the reasons using his fingers. "Beach, sea, storm, and I'm familiar with the area."

"Good enough for me." Paige turned to see Sunny settling into writing mode, her pen moving rapidly across her notebook page.

Sunny looked up and nodded. "The heroine could have a hurricane name."

Booker shook his head and objected. "We might get into gender issues."

Irritation laced through Paige's tone. "Don't resurrect the Battle of the Sexes here, Booker."

"I'm not. I'm being practical. We want a market. No need to antagonize half of it." Heat filled his tone with plenty of indignation and something akin to restrained passion.

Paige questioned her designated role as moderator. "You two are making me dizzy!"

At that point, Booker and Sunny's debate over names started heating up, steam rising from furrowed brows.

Paige pushed her palms down firmly on the table as she stood. "We're making no progress here. Tell you what . . . Here's your assignment for tonight. You two select the names of the hero and heroine. I don't think we need to stick to the hurricane-name idea. Name both MCs. After that, you'll each write a hook line and a scene. We'll see how we can combine them after we share them so we each see what's developing. Hell, I may just do it, too. We've agreed Cape Cod is the setting. We'll reconvene tomorrow. Six a.m. sharp."

Two sets of eyes bored into hers. Both shouted, "What?"

"I can't do that early," Sunny said. "No childcare. My daughter's nanny isn't available until later."

Booker chimed in, "I never do anything before noon except maybe wake up."

Paige threw her hands up. "Fine. We'll compromise and meet midmorning." What else could she say? She was outnumbered. Forcing the issue might mean the real potential of no meaningful work getting done. And Sunny's child competing for her attention wouldn't win Paige any favors.

"I'll try to email you my bits, Paige," Sunny promised. "I suggest y'all try forest bathing this evening. I'm outta here."

"Wait. We should share cellphone numbers." Booker suggested. After everyone exchanged their information, Sunny left.

Booker turned to Paige and asked, "What the hell is forest bathing?"

Paige tapped her foot, still struggling with her agitation and irritation. "Didn't you read the amenities brochures in your cabin?"

"No."

Paige continued tapping her foot. "You walk in the woods and bathe yourself in nature."

"Huh? Why? They have the Spa Haus with a state-of-the-art shower system."

"You have a lot to learn."

"You volunteering to teach me?"

"In a word, No. "

Booker stared at her, looking confused. "I don't see how

walking in a forest has anything to do with our assignment."

Paige simply shook her head. "Men."

She left Booker standing alone, hoping Alex and whatever he was driving waited nearby. She was done with the day and wanted to shut down. After spending time with Tiny, she just might forest bathe herself.

Alex met her in front of the convention center, standing next to a UTV.

Paige raised her hands to her suddenly aching head. "What in heaven's name is this all about?"

Alex grinned. "This chariot is my feeble attempt to get you out in the wild mountain terrain. You need to experience these mountains to fuel the imagination and all that jazz."

"FYI, I spent several hours doing just that this morning, thank you very much."

"Do tell."

"I went up the Space Needle."

"Seriously?"

Paige nodded.

"How'd that happen, boss lady?"

"Booker and the lure of lunch."

"Will wonders ever cease?"

"Is Tiny okay?"

Alex chuckled. "Well, look at you becoming a mutt mama and a tourist after all."

Once Paige reached her cabin, she changed into jeans and a New York Yankees sweatshirt. She donned her Nikes and decided to go in search of the Forest Bathing Trail, intending to let the peace, setting sun, and pine-scented air work their magic.

Once on the trail, she had to admit it did feel good to just *be*. She breathed in the fresh air and the nuances of trace scent released by the forest's dampness. The smell of fresh cedar and hickory enveloped her as she watched the dying sun rays seep through the trees.

She knew she wasn't really upset over their writing triad semi-fiasco. She even acknowledged she wanted Booker and welcomed that bit of Sunny's matchmaking. However, she needed some space to accept the feelings blossoming inside her. Her quest for love was unfolding, and she couldn't ask for more. She briefly closed her eyes and let her body and spirit relax into the evening.

A light mist developed, seeping over the babbling stream and rising to cover the path that looped through the woods. Gradually, the sun's rays disappeared, and moonlight took its place. As she rounded the bend, something in the air, the feel of the place, the energy of the experience, shifted. Alert to the change, she stopped in awe when a solid white buck stole into view. In the sudden stillness, the magnificent stag stood silently in a moonbeam. The wind no longer whispered through the pines, the birds stilled, and even the crickets stopped their song as if the entire forest and its creatures held their breath for a brief moment. As if the world ceased to breathe in the silent, still, magic night. Somehow, magic and majesty melded, and Paige felt she played a part in it all.

The white stag stood stately, regal, big, and seemed all-knowing. Paige swore he winked at her before disappearing into the dark forest.

She hadn't been startled, she realized. She hadn't expected to encounter any wildlife, regardless of how ludicrous that was since she was in a national park, but she wasn't afraid or nervous or worried. Instead, she felt like she had been tested and passed. Renewed, whether by the forest bath, the magic of the moon, or the wonder of the beast, she couldn't say, but she felt calmness and clarity flow through her. Her spirit was at peace, in harmony with nature, and she realized she hungered for life, living, love . . . and food.

The lights of the Lodge's main house lured her inside. A fire blazed in the river rock fireplace. The hand-carved wooden staircase looked warm and inviting. The scent of freshly baked bread wafted in the air, and a buffet was laid out on a long table, but none of that fazed her. What did freeze her, though, was the portrait above the fireplace. Against a dark sky and a full moon stood a compelling image of the animal she had just seen.

Sunny approached, holding a filled buffet plate, and offered it to her. "You look like you've seen a ghost." She smiled. "What's with you?"

Paige swallowed and took the plate. "You'll never believe it, but I just saw that same animal on my forest bath walk." She stood there transfixed on the image and open-mouthed.

"Shut your mouth, Paige." Sunny waved a fragrant slice of bread under Paige's nose. "Seriously, close your mouth. Or at least stuff it. Literally. Take a bite of this home-baked bread. You know seeing the Ghost Stag is good luck, right?"

Paige shook herself out of her daze. "What are the chances . . ."

"Oh, they're very good," Sunny said.

"What?"

"Oh yes. The legend says it's good luck if you see the Ghost Stag and are looking for love. If you see it, you'll find love on the premises, and if you're really lucky, you'll see your future family."

Paige chuckled. "I hope I'm not *that* lucky! A *baby?* Love you say? Here at Sugarlands Lodge?"

"Um-hmm, aren't you the lucky one? Staying in the lucky cabin, seeing the Ghost Stag, and Booker making goo-goo eyes at you to boot."

"Pshaw!"

"For real." Sunny held her hand to cup her ear. "What's that I hear? Wedding bells?" And damned if the mantle clock didn't choose that moment to chime eight bells for the hour.

"What's going on?" a voice like velvet asked.

Booker stood straight, slim, fit, and tall, bathed in the firelight.

Sunny sashayed away. "Wouldn't you like to know?"

CHAPTER THIRTEEN: PURPLE PROSE

Booker returned to his cabin after a short—too short—conversation with Paige next to the fireplace in the Lodge's main building. Although he would have enjoyed spending more time with the feisty woman, he did have a bit more work to do on his assignment.

He pressed *play* on his recorder and listened to what he had recorded earlier. *"Pantene inhaled deeply, trying to enshrine the briny air, sea breeze, surf, and sea and incorporate them within her forever."* He smiled, really liking the name he'd chosen for the heroine. *"She didn't dare exhale lest she let any part of the sea's glory, its majesty, its splendor, and its awesome beauty escape her notice."* A few beats of silence passed before it continued. *"The Atlantic overwhelmed her, embracing her tightly and holding her in its thrall yet filling her with its grace. The sea was as alive as she was. There was nothing tame about this ocean, just like there was nothing tame about her, not her heart, not her soul, not her spirit. It was untamed, wild, pulsating with life and free as Jonathan Livingston Sea Gull."*

He fast-forwarded the recording, bypassing notes to himself in search of something else he had dictated earlier. *"The sea greeted her like a lost love, giving her a rollicking welcome after years apart. It swelled within her soul and made itself at home."* He nodded, liking that bit.

He opened his laptop and got to work. His process of dictating his thoughts, feelings, musings, research, sentences, and phrases into his recorder worked for him. He let those wisps of ideas stew for a while, then wrote. He didn't consider himself a pantser or a plotter. *Guess I'd call myself a hybrid.*

He wrote for several hours, wishing he had a printer. He could send it to the Author's Lair equipment at the Convention Center, but he couldn't get hold of it until the next day. Unless . . . *Hmm, the Lodge must have a printer somewhere . . .* He started to stand but paused when he looked out the window. *Holy Shit, the sun is rising already? Damn, have I written a hook anywhere? I've got a scene and a heroine. What about the hero's name? Brad? Trevor? Rod with a power tool between his legs?* He grinned. *Rod Goodman? Preston Worth? Sawyer Draftsman? How about Rod Hardson. Ooh, I like that one.*

Sunny wasn't worried about their assignment. Yes, she was a writer, but it was her matchmaking role that consumed her at the moment. Based on what she'd observed between Paige and Booker, her matchmaking was coming along nicely. This was no surprise to her since she had gotten the scoop from Alex and Ned, Paige's editor, about Paige.

As a matchmaker, she had sensed Paige's match nearby when she registered. When Booker walked in, she knew immediately he was Paige's other half. She smiled, knowing she had magic and lore and a God-given gift for spotting likely matches. She was a master, a legend at it — at least in her own mind.

On her notebook page, she had scrawled, *"Die, damn it."* She also had character names selected. After watching a few *YouTube* videos, she knew she'd gotten a sense of the Cape Cod setting and how her scene would play out. She was less worried about that, though. She sensed she'd be better off setting the stage for the next scene between Booker and Paige. She needed something to shake things up, sensing things could get heated between them the next time they met. She had a sudden premonition and said, "Siri, call Big Orange Adventure Tours."

Despite the text Paige got from Sunny indicating their mid-morning writing session would take place at Mynatt Park, she got up with the sun as usual. She made a beeline for the freshly brewed coffee available at the Lodge's main house, snatched a yeasty cinnamon bun, and ate it while pondering all that had happened and what might happen later that morning. She thought about her new life goal. *Find a soulmate. Hmm.* She looked up, her gaze caught by the canvas displaying the stag she had spied the night before. She walked closer to the stunning painting of what Sunny called the Ghost Stag. *What do you know, buster? Methinks you're simply oil on canvas, a flesh and blood creature in the moonlight of the forest, but no mystical, magical oracle of love.* Still, the notion niggled at her brain as she walked back to her cabin.

Although she had told the others she wasn't going to write unless asked, she had begun to mentally plot a scene the minute the setting was announced. She, after all, was a plotter, and even though she wasn't familiar with Cape Cod, she did know the Long Island shoreline.

She named her heroine Patience Brewster, and the hero—GQ gorgeous—Captain George Prescott. She retrieved her notes and did something out of character, especially for her, she sat at the desk fully dressed—no comfy PJs, no bunny slippers, just a Lodge to-go coffee mug. She did, however, precisely align her pens, sharpened pencils of equal length, and highlighters on the desk—her usual setup—before she started working.

Although it was still early, Paige texted Alex, reminding him to pick her up at nine-thirty for Mynatt Park's writing session, and set the alarm on her smartwatch to remind herself. Then she wrote undistracted, following her process and not thinking—too much at any rate—about her fellow writers' quirky routines.

An unwelcomed, noisy tone from her cell phone startled her back to reality but reminded her she had places to be. *Shit! I was really in the zone this time.* Her attention switched to getting ready to meet Alex. She unplugged her laptop, ensuring it was fully charged for her writing triad appointment.

Paige threw a poncho over her shoulders, gathered her things, and walked to the main house where she'd meet Alex. Previously, they'd discussed meeting there to prevent Tiny from jumping to any predictable doggie conclusions and causing a canine catastrophe. For sure, Tiny would rush to the door, no doubt expecting to play and accompany her.

She sat in a rocker on the veranda, taking in the peace and serenity of the mountains. Birdsong filled the air, and she heard a woodpecker knocking the heck out of something nearby. She looked for the noisy culprit, and her gaze fell on a huge red-headed bird. She snapped its picture, intending to Google it,

Alex appeared with a key fob and to-go coffee cups in hand. "I got us an epic set of wheels for the rest of our stay." He paused, following her gaze to the bird. "That's a pileated woodpecker. They're prevalent here."

"Do we have them at home?"

"I've heard a knock or two when I walk Tiny in Central Park but haven't seen one. Anything's possible in New York City. I'm excited to see more of this area. Mynatt Park is a short ride from the convention center. At this time of the morning, traffic will probably be heavy, so we'd better get a move on if you want to be on time."

As Alex spoke, a rough, red-eyed version of Booker dragged himself to a chair and sank into it. He scrubbed a hand over his face.

Paige held back a chuckle. "Out late painting the town?"

"Not unless you count writing as partying. I need coffee."

Alex handed Booker a cup and studied him carefully. "You sure you're not hung over?"

"I'm just not a morning person. For me, this is the crack of dawn."

Paige looked at him in surprise. "I guess there really is something to the night owl versus early bird discussion. You sure you can do this?"

"In a word, no," he replied, fatigue heavy in his voice and lack of sleep apparent in his body language.

"Perhaps you should ride along with us. No sense fighting the traffic when you're half asleep."

Booker simply nodded.

Alex chimed in. "Good idea. I have rented new wheels. Ready?"

Booker finished his coffee and then looked around. "Have you guys seen my phone? My glasses?"

Paige couldn't help but laugh. "You're wearing both." She moved in close, lifted the phone that peeked out of his shirt pocket, and then tapped her finger on his nose.

"Huh?"

"Come on." She took him by the crook of his arm and led him into the SUV, where Alex held open a door.

She slowly helped Booker into the back seat and said, "Perhaps I really should have set our meeting an hour or two later."

"You think, boss lady?" Alex chuckled as he slid into the driver's seat.

A soft snore startled Paige. She turned around, shocked to discover Booker had dozed off in the back seat. For heaven's sake, they were barely half a mile from their lodging. She had no experience with late risers and felt bad for suggesting the earlier writing schedule. Sunny surely had to get up early with a young child and all. She hoped so, or not much would get done this session. *I hope the drive to the park will give Booker the extra sleep he needs.*

Paige concentrated on the view instead of Booker, though this emerging side of him cast him in a new light. His sleep deprivation was real and clear to anyone who looked at him. *Wonder how late into the night he wrote? He looks so vulnerable.* Not like the Marlboro Man they had joked about when they met in the pharmacy. Not now, at any rate.

They passed a stand of trees, and a burst of yellow leaves popped against the green conifers. *Fall is so beautiful.* She felt as happy as that snappy burst of yellow. *All's well in my little world.*

Twenty minutes later, Alex announced, "Here we are. Text me your pick-up time. Good writing."

Booker startled awake. Then he yawned and stretched after getting out of the vehicle. Alex drove away, and Booker and Paige started looking for Sunny.

Surprisingly, Sunny discovered she was the first to arrive at the park. She spotted a picnic table nearby, noting that it was in a setting that was just right—not too bright, not too dark, not too hot, not too cold. Located near the restroom and a roofed pavilion, the spot could not be any better. Plus, it was next to a small stairway that led to the parking lot. She heard the hum of an engine and looked up to see Booker exit an SUV, stretching and flexing.

Paige followed suit but beat him to the picnic table. She arranged her laptop just so and placed her yellow legal notepad and perfectly sharpened pencils as if she were setting a table. She appeared ready to write. Sunny raised her right wrist and looked at her watch. It was well after their meeting time, and she was anxious to get started.

Sunny greeted them. "Looks like we're all here. Take a seat. Did you finish your assignment, Booker?" When he nodded, she continued. "I think to be as politically correct and objective as possible, we should read the manuscripts in

alphabetical order by surname. We have Days and Turner."
She pointed to herself, then Booker. "That means you go second, Booker. Sorry about that. Any objections?"

Nobody objected.

Sunny smiled glad to get her part over first. "My characters
are named Siera Simmone and Piere Le Grande."

Booker's face went slack, but no sound escaped him while
Paige's eyes widened.

Sunny took a deep breath and continued. "My hook is *Die,
bitch.*" She proceeded to read her prose aloud.

*"Siera heard the trunk lid crash down on her. So this is what it's
like to get murdered. This is where I die? I don't think so. She undid
the inside latch and threw herself out. She heard the brakes screech,
but she was already rolling down the steep roadside gully. Luckily,
she still had her knife."*

Booker nodded slowly. "Sounds like an elevator pitch.
Plenty of action."

Paige said, "I like the name Siera. What's the hero's name
again?"

"Piere Le Grande."

Booker wrinkled his nose.

"What?"

"Sounds like a mix of Hispanic and French."

"I guess it does. So what?"

Paige tapped a pencil against her temple. "I think what
Booker may be saying—correct me if I'm wrong, Booker—the
names don't sound like Cape Cod ones."

Booker nodded.

"Oh, hmm, I didn't think of that," Sunny reflected. "I just
liked the name *Siera.*"

Paige smiled. "How about these? Patience Baxter. Nathanial Fletcher."

Booker nodded. "I can live with those."

Sunny summed things up. "Okay. We have the setting and
hero and heroine. We still need the hook line to catch the

readers and reel them into the story. We haven't heard much from you, Booker. Do you want to pitch your names and scene?"

"No. I'm fine. Later on, okay with you? I'm happy to listen to you guys, though. What have you got, Paige?"

"I worked from what we had and concentrated on the hook. I think what we came up with yesterday is too wide in scope and needs to be trimmed. Does anyone have those lines?"

Sunny flipped through her notes. "I jotted down what Booker recorded and modified it a bit. Here's what I wrote."

She read it aloud. *"A once-in-a-thousand-year storm, rising seas, a national park, politicians, scientists, and a family beach compound collide at the same time a rogue government ignites a worldwide war."*

Booker winced. "I suppose I have to agree with Paige. That is a lot for a short story."

Sunny drummed her fingers on her pad of paper. "Since we're in a national park, I think we can agree that concept fits. I know how a family-owned property works, so we could keep that element, too."

Paige said, "Your idea of an environmentalist works, too, Sunny. Could Patience be one?"

Booker shifted his weight. "Nathanial could be the politician who wants to preserve the family compound, creating tension between the two. And I can see the grounds for a later compromise. I think the rising sea levels can work because it's set in Cape Cod, but perhaps the *war* should be between nature and progress. You know, environmentalist versus politician, Patience versus Nathanial."

"Works for me." Paige looked satisfied.

Sunny frowned. "Giving up the worldwide war bit all right with you, Booker?"

"I'm fine with it." There was a strange glint in his eyes, though.

Sunny did a double take. "What's that look for, Booker?"

"I think we're ready for my scene. Do you mind if I read you my work?"

Sunny shrugged. "Go ahead."

He pulled out his cell phone. "This scene begins with Pantene —"

"Hold on a second." Paige slapped her forehead. "*Pantene?*" She stared at Booker, her mouth hanging open.

"It was good enough for Victor Hugo."

Sunny furrowed her brow. "Huh?"

Paige squirmed in her seat. "What does he have to do with the name?"

"Fantine was his character in Le Miz. I found it inspiring. Pantene rhymes and sounds nice."

"It's a shampoo."

"I'd name a daughter Pantene."

"You would not."

"Yes, I would."

"I'd never name a daughter of mine —"

"I bet you would if I asked nicely."

Sunny's gaze bounced back and forth between her writing buddies. She almost laughed because they sounded like how she and Storme argued.

Booker shrugged and started reading. "*It was a dark and stormy afternoon. Pantene walked down a set of steps built somehow into the dune leading to Race Point Beach.*"

Paige groaned. "You can't begin with such a cliché. *It was dark and stormy* . . . It's bad writing."

"I said afternoon, not night."

"It's still terrible."

Sunny put her fingers in her mouth and whistled. "Ground rules, beta readers, puh-leeze. Be nice and keep it civil. Constructive criticism only because we're just brainstorming. Nothing's a dumb idea, not even a name. Settle down."

Booker said, "Yeah, chill."

Paige shot him the proverbial *teacher look*. A killer look.

Booker smirked as he started reading again. *"Something deep within Pantene skipped, danced, and pranced its way through her veins. It flowed free and easy, like the sea ebbing and flowing in its perennial dance of life, feeling, hope, joy, and bliss. A soaring that set her passion free, skipping its way across the sea's whiteheads and bringing renewal, peace, love, and joy — a solace for her aching psyche."*

Paige shifted in her seat, folded her hands, took her leopard print readers off, and cleared her throat. She looked like she was preparing to tear into Booker again.

Sunny jumped in before Paige could say anything. "Yowser. Sounds like Booker is taking on a female perspective, demonstrating men can write from a female point of view. Didn't we tell you so?"

Booker scowled, somewhat defensively. "No, I told you. I thought — and still do — that a male's unconscious bias bleeds through the text. What I am reading is me trying to write from a female perspective. I can see you think the attempt stank, confirming what I said all along."

"Aren't you cuter than a basket of kittens . . ." Sunny trailed off and then turned to Paige. "Help me out here."

Paige sighed. "Besides the flowery words, you certainly caught her passion. The passage is almost a sex scene — "

"Yeah, minus the sex," Sunny interjected.

"Huh? Descriptions are important. That's neither male nor female."

Paige appeared to be struggling with what she was about to say, half rising from her seat and leaning on the table. "Let's agree to set the metaphor for sex aside for now. The writing is a flat-out prime example professors would use when defining purple prose."

Booker countered fast. "There's no sex. As Sunny herself pointed out."

"Purple prose is any time there's a hyperbole, a word fest,

an elaborate or ornate long redundant description."

"Like that sentence?" he said with a snarky tone.

Paige just glared at him.

"As I said," he responded, "men write action-packed sentences. They don't do this poetry. I tried, and this is what happened. Although I must say, it was fun to craft that sentence. What's more, Paige, you just proved my point." Now, he also rose half out of his seat, leaning closer to Paige. "Men don't write like women. Therefore, a male could not be writing as Molly Made." He came to a full stop with a shocked expression.

Paige's mouth dropped open.

Sunny spoke in a rush. "What? Why are you talking about Molly Made? Her writing is scorching, and she makes my girlie parts party, but who's talking about her?"

"I meant Mary Ann Evans," Booker grumbled.

"Who?"

"You know. George Elliot. Silas Marner."

Paige stared at Booker, trying to think of a way to make her point without starting another argument. She cleared her throat again, put her readers back on, and grabbed his phone, glancing at the next passage. "Here's another good example of what I mean . . ." She shook her head and started reading.

"Pantene danced with the surf that chased her feet at the shoreline. She sashayed with the seaweed tossed by the strong waves. She do-si-doed with the splash and sea spray created when the sea met the shore, and she laughed with her whole self. In the background, she saw Rod Hardson. But he was not her focus. Being. Just being was thee thing. Being in this moment, in this sea space, listening to the sea crash like sea cymbals against the cliffs, creating an endless sea symphony that she'd never forget.

"That, Booker, is over the top. Another perfect example of purple prose."

"I'm *showing* the scene here, not *telling*."

Paige coughed, raised her brow, and opened her mouth to speak, but Booker jumped in before she could say anything.

He waved at the phone. "Keep reading. You'll like the next line."

Paige read it aloud. "*The ocean rocked her like no man ever had.*"

"See? Tell me that isn't a great line."

A smile tugged at her mouth. *I really like that one.*

Booker folded his arms in front of him. "Admit it damn it. That's a damned powerful sentence."

Paige countered. "It says a lot. This proves my point. A man can write women's fiction."

He hmphed. "If you say so."

Paige peered at him closely. *Why is this an issue? What's going on? Methinks something's up here, but I don't know what.* "I do. Just look at the lines at the book signing. What if Molly Made *is* a man writing as a woman? Plenty of men were standing in her line."

Booker seemed stuck on his point. "They're buying them for their wives."

Sunny laughed. "Keep telling yourself that."

Booker ignored them. "Keep reading is what I say."

Paige sighed. "Just for the record, Booker, there's repetition in this piece. It's redundant."

"Says the pot to the kettle."

Paige wanted to reach out and smack him on the head. Instead, she looked down and started reading again.

"*The sun shone on the sand as if to kiss it good morning. Those early risers were quiet as mice on Christmas Eve. Children still slept. She would, from here on out, know this place not as Cape Cod but as Paradise. Parents greeted each other, careful not to break the morning peace. Their words, just above a whisper, chirped like a lone baby bird's but not nearly so demanding. More like a proof of life. A slice of sound. Not loud. Not soft. Not piercing. Just clear enough to keep the magic going as if acknowledging the sanctity of the space between sleep and wakefulness. The sea and sky are far better than ever, beyond dreams. Gradually, their tousled cherubs awoke, rubbing their eyes as bed-headed parents tended to their children's needs. The sea and sky kissed hello. Rod joined her. He said it all in one word. Awesome."*

Paige smiled wryly. "Rod summed it up in one word —"

Sunny piped up. "Awesome."

"That's my point. One word could do it." Paige continued as if Sunny hadn't chimed in. "However, I'd pick a better word than that. Awesome? Really?"

Sunny added her two cents to the conversation. "I have to agree with Paige about the redundancy and the extreme verbiage."

Booker cocked a brow. "I'm writing a Regency romance. That genre uses rich language."

Sunny looked confused. "Did they have environmentalists back then or rising sea levels? Those issues smack of contemporary romance, not a Regency, bud."

"Fine," he grumbled. "But no one ever specified what *style* of romance we were writing."

"Whatever, but you're right," Paige groused. "As of now, we agree we are writing a contemporary romance."

Sunny smiled, and Booker nodded.

She wondered if anything could lessen this impasse and the tension she felt heating up. She wanted to strangle Booker, and he looked like he wanted to throttle her, judging by his hands clenching then unclenching.

Paige looked at her writing partners and packed up her stuff. "Our time is up for today. Your next assignment is to write a sex scene. Not one using sex as a metaphor but a bona fide sex scene. Then we'll get down to the nitty-gritty writing. We'll meet tomorrow at —"

Ah-ooo-ga!

Something sounding like an old Model T horn distracted

Paige. Booker frowned, but Sunny seemed unsurprised and appeared to know what was going on.

Paige turned to the parking lot and saw the horn attached to a big orange safari jeep.

CHAPTER FOURTEEN: JEEP SWEEP

Paige pulled herself together. "What's going on? Sunny?" Sunny simply smiled and winked. "Trust me."

The driver emerged and joined them at the table. "Howdy, I'm Tony from Big Orange Adventure Tour. I'm here to take" — he looked down at an invoice to read — "*Paige Newhart and Booker Turner* on our Jeep Sweep of the Smokies Tour."

"Huh?" Booker muttered.

"This is our signature vehicle for our tours." He waved toward the orange open-top *Jeep Wrangler*. "Our trip will take us through the Smokies on the Cherokee Orchard Road loop, part of the Roaring Fork —"

"What the heck?" Paige bleated.

If Tony wondered about her and Booker's questions, he hid it well. His smile never faltered as he continued his spiel. "This adventure tour begins and ends here at the City of Gatlinburg's Mynatt Park, the home of the Memorial and Tribute Plaza commemorating the loss of fourteen souls in the 2016 wildfire. I hate to start on such a note, but I'll remind y'all we're mountain-strong and mountain-tough. The memorial is divided between two separate plazas and flanks Le Conte Creek. Down yonder is a footbridge that connects the two plazas with plenty of picnic sites nearby. Y'all can check that out when we return at the end of the tour. The park is undergoing renovation, and we're proud of our new Pickleball field, renovated picnic grounds, and newly paved walkways. Kindly step this way." He led them to the orange 4x4.

Paige could do little but follow, since Booker grabbed her

elbow and tugged her along. Truth be told, she wanted to expound more on her frustration with Booker's writing, but the tour prevented that. She'd come off as peevish and stubborn if she refused the gift of an adventure.

Booker stepped aside when Tony opened the door so Paige could climb into the back seat first, then followed to sit next to her.

Sunny smiled and waved them off.

Her irritation didn't prevent her body's reaction to Booker's toned frame as the jeep wound its way up the mountain and the curves threw their bodies closer together.

She forced herself to focus on the yellow, orange, scarlet, and plum leaves that drifted down like snowflakes and covered the two-lane road. She gasped when she saw the tableau unfold around them. *Words fail me. It's awesome!*

She cringed. She had accused Booker of using that one word. She even claimed she'd have selected another choice, but here she was saying *awesome* herself. *Good grief — life, fate, or karma is trying to keep me humble.*

Still on Cherokee Orchard Road, not long after they set out, Tony stopped near a quaint rustic cabin that looked like it had stepped straight out of a history book. The peace of the place calmed her as they wandered toward the building.

"This is our first stop, the *Noah* Bud *Ogle Cabin*. You'll note it's not a typical cabin, but what's called a *saddleback* cabin because it's two single-pen cabins sharing a fieldstone chimney. Bud added the second cabin after he and his wife, Lucinda, started having young'uns and quickly outgrew the original space. You can tell the two structures by the different heights of the roofs. Covered porches were added to the front and back of the house to expand their living quarters. With eight kids, you can see why space was at a premium."

Paige walked to the windows. "These are glass!"

Tony chuckled. "Like I said, this is not a typical cabin of the time. Bud did well for himself. He supported his family by growing corn and a variety of apples, which he sold to other mountain residents and sent the excess to markets in Knoxville." He winked. "Not saying he had a still, but he had the corn needed for producing moonshine."

Paige nodded. "I guess he could afford the glass then."

"What did the other settlers do, you ask?" Tony said. "They used smaller windows." He laughed. "Some used oiled or heavy waxed paper, even newspaper, though it blocked the light. Many people also used newspaper as wallpaper to insulate their cabin."

Booker examined the walls and door jams. "They didn't use nails."

"Nails were expensive and scarce. Instead, they used handhewn cove wood notched together with half-dovetails to build the cabin. And nature's *Ape Glue.*"

"Say what?" Booker challenged with a lifted brow.

"Yeah, back in the day, they called it pine pitch. Very tarlike and sticky. Did the job."

They walked the grounds looking at the corncrib and a pass-through barn.

Booker revealed how impressed he was at the ingenuity of the settlers. "And we think we invented the drive-through concept. All we modern people did was upgrade the materials. Keeps you humble, doesn't it?"

Tony strolled beside them and nodded his head toward a path. "If you follow that trail, you'll find the tub mill and creek. It's pretty. We have time if you want to take a stroll."

Paige headed that way, and when Booker caught up to her, she said, "At least our garrulous guide didn't tell us to take a hike. Do you think he picked up our tension?"

Booker shrugged. "Naw. Come here."

She looked at him and tamped down the last of her exasperation. She normally never followed that particular demand, but she ambled over to his side. Why exactly, she couldn't say. Still a tad reluctant, she moved with him when he pulled her further into the woods. He tilted her chin and kissed her lips. It wasn't a passionate kiss. It was sweet and soft and very, very nice.

"What was that for?"

"A makeup kiss."

"Never heard of that."

"It's a prelude to makeup sex."

"Subtle, huh?" She laughed. "I just might be up for that."

They walked the rest of the way, comfortable again in each other's company. When they came to the creek, they rock-hopped their way across. The stream meandered a bit, and Paige paused to simply watch the water skip over rocks and race through the trees. She followed it around the bend to see it ultimately flow into a raised flume that fed the tub mill. A posted sign stated corn was once ground there, and the structure now stood in testimony to times gone by. Their walk ended as the trail led them back to the peaceful cabin.

Tony rushed from the porch to meet them. He seemed riled. "I'm darn glad y'all are in one piece."

"Say what?" Booker frowned.

"Didn't y'all see them bears? I was fixin' to call the Rangers! Mama bear and her two babies were wanderin' down that-a-way, where y'all were. I feared they ran y'all up a tree. Or worse . . ." He shook his head. "Mauled yer tails."

Paige shivered. "No. We didn't see them. I thought black bears were not dangerous. We saw a Mama and her four cubs at Sugarlands Lodge."

"You'll probably see more on this leg of the tour."

"Where's the best place to see a bear?" Paige's curiosity got the best of her.

"Chicago." Tony smirked.

"In the zoo?" She laughed. "You got me there." She laughed. "Seriously, though."

"In Kodiak."

Booker grumbled. "I think Paige means here, Tony, not Alaska."

Good Lord! Booker's mansplaining to a man! Geesh.

Tony laughed. "No, Kodiak Bass and Pro in Pigeon Forge has a big ol' black bear. It's located near the *Krispy Kreme* donut dumpster."

"Really?"

"Yeah, most bears go there to get some of them gooey-filled glazed donuts."

She shook her head. "Come on now. You're supposed to be our tour guide, keeping us safe and all that. We're in the wilderness here."

Tony quit laughing. "Just yankin' yer chain. You said you'd seen a Mama Bear with her cubs. Not so tame, they're wild animals that protect their young fiercely." He let his breath out in a whoosh and pulled his hat back on after swiping a hand across his brow. "Best we move on now."

Paige hurried to the Jeep. "What do we do if we meet a bear on the trail?"

"Give 'em a wide berth."

"That's it?"

"Now, I didn't say that . . . If that fails, make yourself big and threatening. Wave your arms. Shout. Throw rocks or sticks, but do not run."

"Why"

"You know dogs?" Tony glanced at her and Booker, and they nodded. "They chase you when you run . . . it's instinct. That's what bears do, too. Y'all running will make you look like prey. Do not run. And do not climb a tree. Bears are better at it than you are."

Neither Paige nor Booker spoke as Tony shifted gears — literally and figuratively — resuming his tour guide tone. "We are turning onto Roaring Fork Road, a one-lane, one-way road also known as *Roaring Fork Motor Nature Trail.*, and we'll be climbing. The terrain is steep, but you'll be seein' more streams, mills, waterfalls, and structures ahead. Keep your cameras ready."

Tony went quiet for a bit, so she and Booker just enjoyed the scenery. Then they came to a line of cars parked so close to the road that Paige wondered if their Jeep could get past them. A little further down the road, they approach a parking lot with trail markers reading *Rainbow Falls* and *Bullhead Trail*.

"Up for a hike?" Tony asked. "The falls are very pretty this time of year with the leaves so full of color."

Paige looked at Booker.

"You wanna hike? Booker asked.

"Hell no! That hike sounds hard. And with the possibility of bears, no way, Jose."

Tony chuckled. "Good call. Those trails are hard. Strenuous. Folks take half a day to get there. We don't have that kind of time, at any rate."

"What if we said we wanted to hike it?"

Tony laughed. "I got a cure for that."

"Oh?"

"I'd remind you about hungry bears filling their bellies for the coming winter and mistaking you folks for dinner."

They laughed.

They continued making their way along the Roaring Fork Motor Nature Trail. Tony made a few brief stops at overlooks, where Paige and Booker could stretch their legs and take in the spectacular views of the Smokies. Their tour was appropriately named. It was a real *sweep* through the Smokies.

Tony continued rattling off more information about the settlers of the area, the homes they left behind, and the daffodils they planted that still bloomed long after their owners and their cabin were gone. He also pointed out other examples of the local flora and fauna.

Paige enjoyed learning about all of it. She was learning

more about Booker, too. From what she gathered, he clearly found the tour information interesting. His questions amazed her, ranging from cabin construction to herbal medicines, the Cherokee Nation, and topography. He insisted they get out at every opportunity to identify a wildflower, bird, or rock formation. She liked the courtly way he helped her mount or dismount from the jeep and push vegetation aside so she could pass safely. He took every opportunity to touch and kiss her. The kisses were short and sweet but packed with heat.

Tony drove further and parked at a breathtaking overlook that made for great scenic photos of the dazzling panoramic view.

Booker slipped his arms around her and sighed. "I think I found my happy place."

"Me too."

Tony didn't say a word—none were necessary. They left only when other tourists needed the parking spot.

A short ride took them to a small parking lot where a white-painted clapboard house trimmed in turquoise stood not too far from the road. Paige was dumbfounded. "Tell me about this house."

Tony parked and obliged her. "This place is known as Alfred Reagan Tub Mill. That's the tub mill standing on the roadside. The house is the only *sawn board* cabin in the area that is painted. Believe it or not, they got the paint from Sears and Roebuck. Back then, they supposedly only had three colors, two of which were white and turquoise. Mr. Reagan was a farmer, blacksmith, carpenter, and preacher who, with his wife, raised seven children. Come along now, we have two things more to do and see."

As they drove through the area, Roaring Fork River kept them company with its clean, clear water, but nothing compared to the site known as *The Place of A Thousand Drips*. They crossed several rustic bridges before they arrived. Like before, other visitors stopped to shoot several pictures. More than one person had a tripod set up, and an artist planted an easel and worked on canvas.

Tony launched into a mini lecture as they got out of the vehicle to take in the view. Paige was enthralled, not by the information, but by the tingle and gentle music the stream made as it traced its way down from a steep cliff. Booker made the short climb to her side.

She nestled into his chest. "This is my favorite spot. I found my thrill among Le Conte's hills."

Hand in hand, Paige and Booker followed Tony back to board the jeep. In less time than it took to shake a leg, Tony pulled into parking by some rustic unpainted wooden structures named *Elys Mill*. Paige noticed beehives out behind the structures. The shop offered cider, donuts, and lemonade. It was filled with a variety of interesting and fun hand-crafted items. A woman, presumably an Elys, sat working an old-time spinning wheel, chatting with some tourists as Paige picked up some honey and Booker grabbed a few guidebooks. The woman at the spinning wheel apologized to her listeners and approached the register, giving Paige and Booker a warm smile after ringing them up, then returned to her guests.

Booker swallowed the last of his cider. Paige couldn't help but appreciate the picture he made as he drank. There was something rugged, primitive, and sexy about it. She felt it in her core, where heat pooled.

Once they were back in the jeep, Booker said, "That was a wonderful end of a remarkable journey."

"Oh, it's not over just yet," Tony announced. "Only one last adventure to go." He drove the East Parkway for a bit, got off on Baskins Creek Bypass, then hit some back roads, judging by the lack of traffic and the road conditions.

When they reached a rugged forested track lined with hemlock, white oak, maple, and tulip trees, Tony said, "Did I tell you this tour includes a deep tissue massage?"

"Uh, no," Paige and Booker said at the same time.

"Yes, it's our *hill*billy special. It's about to start. Better use the grab bars," Tony announced, "We're going off-roading. Hold on!"

Suddenly they were off, racing through the rough terrain and bumping into each other as Tony plowed ahead. At first, the road was rutted and gravelly, but they soon found themselves flying over grass, going down ravines, up hills, rushing through streams, bumping, jostling, and bouncing their way, laughing and screaming.

Once going over a particularly hilly and rocky crest, Booker yelled, "Yeehaw! That's what I'm talking about!"

"I'm glad you enjoyed our hillbilly massage." Tony chuckled. "You'll feel the results for days. With the tours, we get them daily. Guess you could say we're all over the hill now."

True to his word, Tony drove them back to Mynatt Park. They were happy to leave Tony a generous tip, and he got the last laugh as he handed them a patch that read *I saw a bear on an Orange Jeep Sweep.*

Booker helped Paige out of the jeep. She slowly made her way on wobbly legs to a picnic table, sank onto the bench, and texted Alex.

Come and get us now, please.

Chapter Fifteen: Meanwhile Back at the Spa Haus

Paige rubbed the small of her back as she gingerly stepped out of the SUV once they reached the Lodge. "We need the Spa Haus."

Booker groaned and nodded. "That was definitely an adventure. Tony was a hoot, but my poor aching back. I'll meet you there in an hour."

"Why the wait?"

"Bear needs me."

Paige smacked her forehead. "I'm a bad mutt mama. How could I forget about the dog?"

Alex chuckled. "You have me taking care of Tiny, which gives you a pass. He's fine. But Booker, Bear is pining for you."

Booker instantly looked worried.

Alex held up a hand. "Oh, don't get your boxers in a wad, Booker. Storme Knight opened your cabin so I could take her for a walk with Tiny. They're getting along great. I think they're in love."

Paige laughed and then made a face. "Ouch, even laughing hurt. How am I going to deal with Tiny when I'm so sore?"

This time, Alex laughed. "I took them on an extremely long walk. We covered the entire route from the Sugarlands to the Welcome Center in Gatlinburg. We got back just before you texted me, so they're pretty worn out."

"Alex, you are a genius."

He grinned. "I know."

Paige entered her cabin while Booker and Alex headed toward theirs. She was glad she had the time to spend with her dog. She hated to admit it, but it felt nice to have someone dancing for joy and whirling around just because she existed. She scrubbed Tiny's belly and crooned, "Who's a good boy?" She rivaled Frank Sinatra and Bing Crosby as she plied her dog with love.

Finally, Tiny circled three times and then plopped down on the braided rug. She noticed a large raw bone lying beside the dog. *That should keep him happy. The staff here sure aims to please.*

Paige laughed at the scene, put on her swimsuit and comfy leisure suit, then slipped into her hands-free sneakers, ready to set out for the Spa Haus. She felt secure knowing Alex would stop by the cabin to let Tiny out so he could enjoy his creature habits. Tiny didn't stir as she slipped out of the cabin, but he sure did snore up a storm.

Paige strolled through the colorful autumn-hued leaves, appreciating the beauty wherever she looked. Her walk almost felt sensual. Some colors were vivid, while others displayed soft autumnal pastels. Golds contrasted with the peach, apricot, and pumpkin orange leaves that had fallen on the path. The leaves scattered as she walked. Just before she made it to the fork in the walkway, a few apricot leaves twirled in the gentle breeze, dancing in the air as they leisurely drifted to the ground.

Once she arrived at the Spa Haus, she entered through the purple door and headed to the jacuzzi. She shed her loungewear and slipped into the welcoming water, releasing a soft sigh. *Feels good.* She moved slowly with caution and care because her joints were stiff and sore after the jolting adventure ride. Despite her mere forty-eight years, she felt the strain in long unused muscles.

She reveled in the bliss of the heated water's caress and the experience of this level of comfort. Just what she needed. A respite from her ceaseless, hectic work life. To relax in the low lights of the Spa. To hear the mellow piped instrumental music, To inhale and smell the eucalyptus, and feel the bubbly hot water soothe her aching body. *If this is what living is, I like it. Why am I working my life away?*

She sighed, relaxing in the pleasant surroundings and reviewing the past few days. *I've done so much in such a short time. I have to admit communing with nature has its merits.*

From the beginning of her trip she had experienced more than ever before, to say the least. She hadn't had time to process it all. The stimulation of travel, the surprise of Booker, the success and thrill of her keynote address, the book signing, the splendor of the Smoky Mountain setting, plus the beauty of fall in the mountains with the panoramic views were all almost too much to take in.

After a while, Paige feared her skin might turn into a prune but pushed the worry aside. She basked in feeling relaxed and was nearly in a dream state when Booker — wearing a swimsuit this time — eased his fit-tight body into the jacuzzi.

He slid into the hot water with an elaborate sigh of either relief or pleasure. She wasn't sure which, but the sounds he made turned her on like a light switch, making it hard to rein in her erotic thoughts. She had already experienced hot tub sex, and while she yearned for more, she preferred a less vulnerable setting. They did not have a private party scheduled. Other guests could join them at any time. She'd enjoyed his attention during the Jeep Sweep adventure but desperately needed a bed for any additional escapades. Fortunately for her — judging from how Booker entered the water — he'd prefer a romp in a good old-fashioned comfy bed, too.

She smiled, commiserating with him and moving so he could sit comfortably with her on the seat. "This will fix what ails ya."

"Yeah? Are you sure about that? I ache all over."

"I could help take your mind off of that."

He looked at her with a questioning gaze. "How so?"

She kissed him, feeling his lips respond in kind. She decided she didn't need a bed and no longer needed privacy so much after all. She ran her hands across his pelvic bones, dipping low in search of his rod, when she heard the tinkle of laughter behind her. Several authors she recognized but did not know entered the room and slipped into the adjacent pool.

Booker shrugged and said, "Damn."

She leaned closer and whispered, "Later."

"Right. Good." Booker cleared his throat as they shifted apart slightly. "We have some homework to do."

She turned to face him, tilting her head a tad to the side. "We do?"

"Yeah. You gave us an assignment."

"That's right. Write a sex scene. Hmmm . . ."

"Looks like we can't do that here, but we can talk plot points."

"Will it include a hot tub?"

He poked her in the ribs. "It could."

"Or a shower scene?"

He looked at her through narrowed eyes. "We could conjure up a waterfall scene with two lusty lovers out, uh, loving nature."

"And each other." She got carried away in her head with a scene of two lovers entwined behind a spray of water similar to what they'd seen on their tour when they reached —

Booker snapped his fingers, breaking into her musing. "Let's set Patience and Nathaniel somewhere like the Place of a Thousand Drips. Cape Cod has numerous niches that could work for that."

"Yeah, okay. We'll need to give them some privacy."

"Make sure we add in a ledge, cave, or a cliff."

"A ledge. Why?"

"They're going to be standing. There's moss. He could fall."

"So could she."

He nodded. "If we have a pool below, that would make a splash."

"I see what you did there. That could be fun. Why don't we give them a ledge to play with and then—"

"She falls, and he dives in after her . . ."

"Let's switch it up. *He* falls, and she dives in to rescue him."

"Let's have them dry off around a fire . . ."

"Can't have a fire now. There's a drought."

" I'm talking fiction."

"They could be near a campsite and have a comfy cot and a legal campfire."

"Naw. Too many people."

"Could be an interesting plot development. Builds sexual tension."

"Yeah." He looked at her hungrily.

She returned the look. "Your cabin or mine?"

"Yours has people in and out."

"Right. "

"Let's go."

"We can combine work with pleasure."

"That's my kind of homework."

"But we can't have a fire. Burn ban because of the twenty-sixteen wildfire, remember?"

"We don't need an actual fire. We're both pretty hot right now, wouldn't you say?"

Paige giggled. "Affirmative. Okey-Dokey. Oops, my mind got confused for a second. Our story is not set in the *Smokies*. They're in Cape Cod."

"Yep. They allow bonfires in Cape Cod, and the ocean must have something we can play around with."

They scrambled out of the water and raced to dress. Paige

had never dressed so quickly, like a wildfire was nipping her heels. A fire between them that had kindled when she first met Booker was turning into a full-out blazing inferno. He certainly created a storm of want, need, and desire within her body, her blood heating at the mere thought of their upcoming connection. A fire hot enough to last a lifetime, and she didn't want to ever extinguish it.

It all began with Booker's heated looks, the tingling she felt when her skin met his, and the warmth between them when they brushed against one another. The heat pooling in her girlie parts made her anxious. The flame in his eyes was enough to melt her core. She practically panted for him. Never had she wanted anyone more. She couldn't wait to feel his tongue dancing across her body, seeking to attend to *her* hot spots. She needed him inside her as quickly as possible. She jammed her feet into her slip-ons and fairly flew outside.

Booker didn't appear to have wasted any time as he followed her. His shoes were untied, his socks were thrust in his pockets, and his sweatshirt was inside out and hanging half on, half off. He grabbed her by the hand and hurried her down the path, leading the way to his cabin. He stopped abruptly, shushing her when she nearly stumbled over rhododendron roots.

He pointed forward and whispered, "Oh, my God! Look at that."

She followed his glance and froze. The animal she spotted was more frightening than a mere bear in the woods.

Chapter Sixteen: Something to Tell

A head, poised against the backdrop of the moon, stood the albino stag, looking like he did in the painting over the fireplace at the Lodge.

"The Ghost Stag!" Paige couldn't believe her eyes. She gulped.

The magnificent stag didn't bolt away, didn't move. He simply stood regally as if he was there by appointment and appeared to wait purposedly until he was sure both humans saw and acknowledged him. Then he carefully, slowly walked right smack in front of them, looked them directly in the eye, then pawed the ground before turning to melt into the night.

Paige stared at Booker.

Booker stared at her.

"Uh- oh," was all Booker said just as she echoed him.

Paige grabbed Booker's hand and pulled him toward her cabin, since it was closer. Once inside, she raced to the fireplace mantlepiece, not because she was cold and wanted a cozy fire, but because she was frantic to find a brochure or placard like she'd seen in the lobby. "Look for a pamphlet or something about the stag." Sunny had told her about the stag . . . but it was possible there was a pamphlet about it in every room and cabin of the Lodge.

Booker scrambled, looking here and there, raising tour guides and other brochures. "I can't believe we saw the legendary Ghost Stag."

"Together. Don't forget, we were together. Where's that

damned card anyway?"

Booker tossed the bedcovers aside. "I'm beginning to think the legend is no myth. That was no accident. He was waiting for us." He shoved some clothes aside. "Aha! Found the fucker."

"Read it."

He opened the brochure and scanned it. "Here's what the legend says. "Yadda, yadda, yadda . . . *if two lovers together see the Ghost Stag, united they shall forever be.*"

"You just adlibbed that."

He winked. "That's the gist of it."

"Are you going to propose then?"

"Could be."

"Marriage? Because we saw a deer? And a legend says so?"

"No. Because I love you."

"You do?"

"Yup."

Before she could stop herself, a crazy word popped out of her mouth. "Ditto."

They stared at each other.

"Must be a double dose of Smoky Mountain magic that Sunny keeps yammering about," Paige said.

"You complaining?"

"Not me."

She started tearing at his clothes as he lifted her top over her head. He enveloped her with his arms in a way that was primal, raw, natural, and most definitely satisfying. He pressed the whole of him against her with a low growl as he lowered them to the bed.

When he holds me like this, it's everything I've ever wanted. The whole love thing. Comfort. Passion. Love. Peace. Paradise. Yes. Please. She sighed, then said, "This is just right."

"Excuse me?"

"Perfection. Feels good."

"Passion looks good on you, lady."

As normal—as if anything was normal about this—Paige took the lead. She initiated the hot kisses as she weaved her fingers through his long locks until she reached the rim of his ear, where her tongue took over.

"Whoa, Paige, what's the rush?"

"I want to learn your body. Every part of it." She winked and grabbed hold of his very ready shaft.

"My parts, thank you."

"Looks like your *part* is saluting me, sailor."

He chuckled. "I'd say you got a rise outta me."

"I feel like someone in a Fairy Tale."

"You do? Why?"

"Cuz Goldilocks was right when she said the fit was *just right.*"

"Goldilocks, huh?"

"Shut up and kiss me." She pushed him down against the mattress and straddled him, guiding his hard length inside her with one hand while teasing his sacks with the other. She didn't need much foreplay after all the jostling of their bodies and touching they managed during the Jeep Sweep.

She rode him to the moon and back, then he flipped her and rode her to Jupiter and beyond the blazing path they both now called love. In minutes, they exploded together in a rhapsody she had never experienced before. Booker fell to the side, leaving her panting almost too hard to fully enjoy her afterglow.

Booker seemed to catch his breath before her and rolled to his side, leaning on an elbow and giving her a quick kiss. "Guess we did our homework after all."

She giggled. "Think we can write that up for tomorrow's writing session with Sunny?"

"Well, I'm not sure. Maybe we can add a move here and there."

She purred. "Like what?" Beads of anticipation rolled in her belly, and her breath caught in her throat.

"Like so." He kissed her while slipping his hand between her thighs, his finger finding her clit and playing with it until shudders ran through her body once again. Then he slipped two fingers inside her, and she combusted in his arms.

When the aftershock passed, she muttered, "Write that up, will ya?"

"Why me? Why not us?"

"I'm utterly spent. I emailed you some notes I made before we met up. Feel free to use them." She drifted away, slipping into dreamland.

Booker heard Paige's soft snores and chuckled softly, feeling a bit proud of his part of her exhaustion. "Guess it's up to me to complete our assignment. We're going to get an A-plus on this homework." *Hell, Cinderella fell asleep before I could ask her to the Ball. Oh well, there's still time.*

He got up with care, dressed much more slowly than he had earlier, slid out the door as quietly as a mouse, and began dictating the scene into his recorder as he walked back to his cabin.

By time he reached his cabin he had finished the scene, but he didn't think he would have the balls to read what he dictated aloud to Paige and Sunny. It was hot—verging on porn—so he decided to type it up and email it to them instead. *Though it's triple X-rated, it's bona fide, and I think I did us justice with the assignment.* Then he checked his unopened email and saw the comments Paige had posted earlier. She suggested that the most dominant, most active partner's point of view should be the winning ticket. His eyes nearly bugged out of his head when he read what she had written before their Jeep Sweep adventure. *Holy Shit! My stuff is tame in comparison.* He found it interesting that she wrote her contribution from Patience's point of view while he wrote his scene from Nathanial's. *Wonder what Sunny will say when she gets these? Revisions ought to be interesting.*

Then Bear's barking, jumping, and joyous reaction to his presence had to be acknowledged. He rescued his pampered pooch from her plush doggie bed inside her doggie palace — aka custom-made pink crate. He accepted her thousand doggie kisses and patted the pillow beside his. Bear turned three circles and cuddled into the pillow next to his ear. He smiled as he slid into sleep.

Booker awoke earlier than usual to meet Bear's needs. After taking care of feeding and walking her, he headed to the Lodge, where he intended to order the Mountain Man breakfast and hoped to find Paige.

The waitress told him Paige had been the first patron there that morning. Then she asked if he was sure it was the breakfast menu he wanted since it was nearly lunchtime. *Oh right. Paige wakes at the crack of dawn.*

"I'm a night owl and wake up late, so I'd like the breakfast menu if that's okay."

She nodded and went to swap the menu, returning after a minute or two.

After a quick glance, he said, "I'm craving your Mountain Man breakfast." He handed the menu to her and stopped her before she left to place the order. "Did you happen to notice where Paige went after she ate?"

"She read her phone and then met with Sunny, and they made a ruckus before rushing outta here."

"Huh?"

"Their heads were bent over their phones, and they carried on blushing, whooping, and laughing. I reckon something on their phone got them all riled up."

As he took a sip of coffee, he heard the ping of an incoming email on his phone. He promptly spit his coffee out when he read the email attachment. After he recovered and mopped himself up, he was the one blushing over the piercing thrusts, the impaling cock, and the dripping . . . was that the C-word? He didn't know women thought in those kinds of images. His fingers flew across the keyboard when he added a flaming, throbbing, firm dick here and there while he contemplated a hot bathtub scene.

When his phone pinged again, he found his own cock dancing in his pants. He turned his attention to his breakfast and began eating the sausage. He licked his lips and thought about the taste of Paige's—and her nether set, too—then added a pant-worthy ending to the scene, much like their last encounter. He decided to have a second and third cup of coffee while he waited for the circus tent in his slacks to die down.

"I presume you'll be at the Fairy Tale Masquerade Ball?" Paige asked as she put her cell phone down.

"Sure am, ma'am. Fiddle-dee-dee." Sunny winked. "Can you guess who I'm gonna be?"

" A curly-headed Scarlett O'Hara. Cute choice."

"Yup. Only Sunny style."

"Huh?"

"I'm going with Carol Burnette's version."

Paige laughed. "Complete with curtain rod?"

"Maybe, or just the red Carol Burnette hair."

"You are a hoot, girlfriend."

"Yes, I am. Jesse's going as Rhett Butler."

They laughed.

"That will get tongues wagging like Bear's and Tiny's when they see us again after a full day of writing."

Sunny gave an exaggerated wink ala Carol Burnette. "Who are you goin' as?"

"I'll give you a hint. Glass slipper." Paige sighed. "If only I had some."

"Cool. Will Booker be Cinderfella?"

"Time will tell. Booker and I haven't talked about it. I don't even know if he's going to the ball at all. The dude is my polar opposite."

"But opposites attract."

Paige simply looked at her. "Sunny, Booker's morning starts at noon, he writes by the seat of his pants and can never find his notes. Need I go on?"

"But he's a prince of a guy." Sunny poked Paige's arm. "Duh, girl. I'm a matchmaker. He's right smack in front of your face. And he's charming."

"Ha, ha. Cute."

Sunny slapped her forehead. "Got it. Let me make a call."

In seconds, Sunny whipped through her contacts and made a call. She must have used the speaker phone, because Paige heard every word as a series of Q and As ensued.

"Merry and Gabbie play princess, right?" Sunny asked.

"Affirmative." A female voice rang in the air.

"Tiaras, heels, scepters, wands, the whole bit?"

"Yes."

"Your girls have big feet, right? We need the glass slippers."

The voice, which Paige finally recognized as belonging to Sunny's twin, Storme, squealed and grumbled.

Sunny looked at Paige's feet, gesturing for her to raise one. She covered the phone against her chest. "About size five?"

Paige nodded.

"Have the girls find 'em for me. Paige needs them."

"Who?"

"Paige Newhart."

Another scream floated in the air.

"You heard me. Yes. She needs them for the ball tonight."

"What ball?"

"I told you about the Fairy Tale Masquerade Ball. It's

tonight. We need a set of glass slippers."

Paige was treated to a vigorous dialogue in what she'd heard called *sister-speak,* a language only the Weathers sisters spoke.

"You did not."

"Did to tell you.

"Did not.'

"Uh-huh."

"Nuh- uh"

Paige's head started bouncing between the words like a pickleball, making her dizzy.

Sunny ended the call. "My sister has two little girls with big feet. Today's your lucky day. We have glass slippers— well, vinyl but they'll work. The girls are into all things princess lately. You've now got shoes, Cinderella."

Paige smiled. Then she left for her cabin. Her plans included a soak in the Spa Haus pool, followed by a hot shower. She wondered whether she could get her fine hair into a bun.

CHAPTER SEVENTEEN: THE BIG LIE

Booker lost himself in deep thought as he got ready for the Fairy Tale Masquerade Ball. *Damn, I didn't get a chance to ask Paige about the stupid ball. I bet she'd be attending. I should have asked her. Maybe it's better this way? Who knows? I intended to keep a low profile while I'm here. Don't want anyone to catch on to who I am. It's getting harder and harder to maintain a hidden identity. It may sell books, but sometimes the pretense gets old and in my way. Especially now that I'm serious about Paige. When do I fess up and tell her who I am?*

He dressed in a pair of white tights, a cummerbund, and a short brocade jacket, groaning as he stalked across the hotel room and peered in the mirror. It was hard not to laugh. He released something between a sigh and a grin. *I look like a ballet dancer or a fourteenth-century fop.* He plunked the fake gold crown on his brow and grumbled. *The things I do for love, but a prince always seems a good choice for a costume ball.*

He took Bear outside to relieve herself and made sure to fluff her plush pillow bed in her puppy palace before he set out to retrieve his vehicle, sighing deeply. He headed to the Gatlinburg Convention Center and parked in the Airport Road lot.

At the last possible minute, he added the white silk mask, took a deep breath, and entered the building. When he walked in, a sign and velvet rope path guided him to the Fairy Tale Masquerade Ball. As he entered, he saw they had opened the divider between Ballrooms A and B, making the space more of a realm than a room. Large French doors that he hadn't noticed before were open to the night, creating a beautiful blend of warm autumn beauty with the light spilling brilliantly from huge crystal chandeliers.

He glanced around the crowded room, spotting servers in medieval livery carrying champagne or some similar brew in flutes or goblets on discreet silver trays. Others had what appeared to be finger foods. Writers in a variety of costumes of familiar fairy tale characters filled the room. All seemed wigged, crowned, or hooded, and most importantly, masked in an attempt to hide their identity. For a group of well-known and seasoned authors, that was tricky business.

The myriad of costumes featured everything from huntsmen to kings, servant girls to queens, swans and satyrs, stags and stallions. Plenty of princesses mingled with knights in shining armor. Toads and frog costumes competed with mermaids and dragons. It was a sight to see. *Seems like anything goes.* He wondered whether Paige would be among peasant girls, princesses, fairies, witches, and crones or perhaps come as the Queen of Hearts.

Paige surveyed herself in the mirror. *Alex outdid himself.* He had packed two gowns. One she had okayed. The other was a surprise. It was perfect for Cinderella. It was an off-shoulder, two-toned baby blue full-skirted affair complete with a draped overskirt straight out of Walt Disney's Cinderella. It fit her like the long elbow-length gloves she now wore. She added a pearl choker to her neck. *All I need is tweeting bluebirds and cute little mice dressed in kerchiefs and skirts.* She carefully added the crowning touch, a satin blue ribbon, to her hair. Slipping into her glass slippers made her laugh. *These plastic kitten heels, complete with a bow, are just what the outfit needed.* Paige snatched the feather-light stole and answered the knock at her cabin door. Mercifully, Tiny had not accompanied her footman, Alex.

He bowed from the waist and spread his arms. "Your carriage awaits, m'lady." He extended his arm to hand her down the few steps to the *carriage*, which was Craig Knight's monster truck.

She sounded like one of Cinderella's spoiled stepsisters as she screeched. "How in heaven's name am I supposed to get into this thing?"

Alex quickly responded by pulling a fold-up set of steps out of the bed of the truck just as any good footman in any fairytale would. She placed her hand in his and climbed in. She needed Alex's help to tuck her dress into the carriage.

The whole situation had her laughing. "Eww, no, don't let me laugh, I'll ruin my make-up."

"Okaaay. Any other instructions, m'lady?"

"Get me back by midnight. Maybe this truck will turn into a regular old roomy SUV before then."

Alex chuckled and whisked her off to the ball. It took some doing to get her out of her carriage, but Alex performed his footman duties admirably with little complaint. Once she had both feet on the ground, he handed her a white beaded satin mask, and voilà, her masquerade was complete. Alex offered his arm and escorted her inside.

She stepped into the entryway festooned with velvet ropes and strands of fairy lights. Dancing LED balloons glittered in almost every nook and cranny. She approached the table by the entrance to the ballroom, greeted by flashing cameras, and handed a small card on which she wrote *Cinderella*. She was given a numbered wristlet dance card.

A herald in fine livery greeted her in the doorway and asked for her name card. Then he turned and announced her arrival in a booming voice. "Milords and ladies, may it please the court. I present Cinderella."

A round of applause welcomed her as she stepped into the ballroom. She barely recognized the place. Even the floors gleamed. The room was ablaze with lights spilling from great chandeliers, wall sconces, ropes of fairy lights, and tea lights. It looked like a fairyland of fire and ice. Crystal leaves dangled from clear, lit trees in the center of white linen-covered tables. However, enough darkness served as a contrast to the light, giving the room a romantic feel. All in all, the ambiance was beautiful to behold.

Paige looked for a tray of champagne flutes, but none were nearby. All she needed was music, a drink, and a man. She surveyed the room. Princes, knights in shining armor, pirates without peg legs, pages, footmen, huntsmen, and even wicked satyrs roamed the ballroom floor. An abundance of choices in a target-rich environment, which should make it easier to find . . . well, a target. A potential mate. Before she could think much about that, a red-headed Carol Burnette Scarlette O'Hara stepped up to the podium.

After tapping the microphone a few times, repeating *testing, testing,* and a few more taps on the mic, Sunny greeted the crowd. "Howdy, y'all. Welcome to the Fairy Tale Masquerade Ball. There are a few things I want to share with y'all. First off, I'm so glad you are here." Sunny's eyes sparkled behind her mask as she scanned the room, "I'm delighted to see the creativity of your costumes. This event contributes to the success of this venture. As many know, the proceeds from your tickets will contribute to a very worthy cause. I'm also happy to announce that Dolly Parton has agreed to match those proceeds for her Imagination Library, her literacy project for children. If you give a child a book, you hook them into reading, thus opening the door to future success. Thank you for your generosity." Turning ever so slightly in the direction of a group of men hovering near the bar she said, "Gentlemen, since we don't have many of you in our romance writer community, we want to thank you for your participation and hope you will favor the ladies here and fill their dance cards."

She gave an exaggerated wink. "This may be the only time you're allowed to have more than one partner."

A nervous twitter filled the room, and several ladies fluttered their fans. Paige was not so sure about dancing with so many men, but she relaxed once she realized it gave her plenty of opportunities to reach her man-target goals. Then she remembered that Booker loved her and smiled. She already had her man.

Sunny continued with her announcements. "Tonight, we will get the results of the judging for the Writers Triad Challenge. The winning trio's story will not only be published in our anthology but will also be adapted as a screenplay for a short movie to be featured at the Sundance Film Festival. We also have not one but two Mystery Guests featured tonight, so be sure to stay until the end of this magical affair." She waved a hand toward the dark stage where silhouettes of the musicians could be seen. "And now, without further ado, I'm pleased to introduce our first Mystery guest. Please put your hands together to welcome Mr. Master Fiddler himself, Caleb Weathers!"

A spotlight singled out a man on the stage, who played a few measures on his fiddle, and then the band joined in with a jaunty tune. Hoots and hollers erupted through the crowd, sounding like a country hoedown despite their fairy tale costumes.

When the song ended and the wild applause calmed down, all the eligible men in the room—those without partners attached to their arms—began circulating the crowd of waiting women. Some wandered with pens in hand to sign dance cards, while others skipped the card and simply asked a fair maiden to dance. Still others approached fair damsels, luring them to participate with flutes of champagne.

Sunny tapped on the mic again, bidding everyone to enjoy the ball. "Let the wild rampage rage."

That was apparently the cue for the disc jockey to spin his discs and start the party by playing a Coldplay tune. His repertoire seemed to include everything from a Strauss waltz to Tina Turner and Taylor Swift. Paige found herself tapping her toes and chomping at the bit, finding it difficult to sit still when the music thrummed through her body. Numerous dance partners approached, and she danced with everyone from Robin Hood to Humpty Dumpty. When a certain fit man wearing man tights asked her to boogie, she accepted with a giggle. Soon, though, the tempo changed to a mellow *Lady in Red* rendition.

"And who might you be?" she asked her partner.

"If I told you —"

"You might have to kill me?" She laughed. "I've heard that line before. I think I may have a clue to your secret identity."

"Well, I know who you are."

"Do you now?"

"I'm quite a fan of your work, *Celebrity MD*. There's a certain magic about you, Cinderella."

She laughed. "Good guess but hardly my secret identity. How about some clues about you?"

"You might not like what I have to tell you." He peered deeply into her eyes after adroitly dipping her. "Mystery feeds the magic. I believe you must be the secret princess."

"And you must certainly be Prince Charming."

"I certainly hope so. I'd like to be *your* Prince Charming."

"Is there anything stopping you?"

"Just a case of secret identity. You have to guess who I am. By the way, you look ravishing. Did your footman fall over in a stupor when he saw you?"

She giggled. "No. He remained the perfect gentleman. But believe me, it was hard to get into this get-up."

"I'll gladly help you get out of your costume."

She laughed and fluttered her lashes. "I just bet you

would." She drew closer to him and rested her head on his shoulder as the music shifted to an even more dreamy tune. "Everyone here has a secret identity. That's the point of the evening, isn't it? A little mystery to figure out just adds to the intrigue of the event, right?

"I hope you feel that way at the crack of midnight." His deep tone and smooth voice caressed her ear. "No telling what might happen when the masks come off."

"Are you afraid I'll turn into a church mouse?"

"I could be the rat from Tchaikovsky's Nutcracker," he warned.

"Ahem, I think you mean the Mouse King. He wasn't a dirty rat." She snickered. "More like just a nut."

She enjoyed their repartee, and truth be told, she loved being in his arms. She inhaled his crisp, clean citrus scent and perfect male pheromones that enveloped her. She breathed deeply, wanting to learn his body through every sense she had. She liked his hard, broad chest, the strong arms encircling her, and the hands that held hers. With her breasts pressed into his chest, she could feel her nipples bead and begin to throb. The closeness of their hips clearly indicated he was responding in kind as she registered his man part throbbing against her stomach.

She mentally shook herself to get the conversation back on track. "Maybe you are a nut. But I'm more afraid you'll turn tail and run like your namesake." She needed some space, some air, a bed, *something*. "The only thing that'll make me run is Molly Made."

He stumbled, flubbing a step, but regained it in a heartbeat. "Why do you say that?"

"We're rivals."

"It'd make some good press if he happened to show up."

"He? Molly's a *she*."

"Of course. My mistake. Maybe you'd like Molly Made if

you gave her the chance."

"I doubt it." She huffed. "Why hide behind all the mystery?"

He shrugged. "Marketing. Sales. Clicks and likes on social media. Take your pick."

"Hasn't she sold enough already?" she grumbled. "I don't want to talk about her anymore. "

He looked at her closely. "Bear with me here, but what if she's a he?"

She laughed outright. "Ha! That'd be the day. We've beat this horse to death. Look how few men are here. No one can get into a woman's psyche like she can. She's a woman, all right."

"Pseudonyms, my dear, may I remind you of Mary Ann Evans, aka George Elliot. Anything's possible."

Their conversation stopped when Caleb Weather stepped forward with his fiddle, and strains of *Turkey in the Straw* changed the tempo.

"You up for this one?" he asked.

She fanned her face. "Not quite. I think I need a drink and some cool air."

He escorted her to the Ogle Terrace and into the moonlit night. The cool air caressed her as they stood silently gazing into the trees with their muted colors.

Not long after, he kissed her softly. "I don't want anything to change this night. This" — he waved his index finger in the space between them — "feels like the real thing."

A flurry of activity drew Paige's attention away from him, his kisses, and his presuppositions. A gal broke in between them. She stepped backward to accommodate the woman.

"There you are!" The woman heaved a sigh. "I've been looking for you everywhere. If you hadn't texted me your costume, I'd still be looking for you, Max. Quick sign and initial this contract." She pointed to the paper. "Sign here and initial where I have the arrow stickies. This has to be received by midnight tonight or — "

Prince Charming grumbled, "It turns into a pumpkin, I know, I know."

"It goes to the next bid," the woman grumbled as she flipped the pages.

Prince Charming scowled and barely looked at the document. As he handed them back to the girl, Paige noticed MM written with a flourish filled the page, reminding her of something . . . but then it hit her in the face. *I've seen that scrawl before. Oh, my God.*

In a heartbeat, the implications of those two simple letters of the alphabet slammed into her like a Mack truck. The force of her realization ripped the air from her lungs. She couldn't breathe. The enormity of it swamped her and turned her inside out. Her head swam with flashbacks of banners and book signings, images of bookmarks and swag filled her mind's eye. *How could I be so blind? How come I didn't see this coming? Two little initials have overturned all my dreams of finally finding my hero. Booker is royal, all right, a royal pain in the ass. Prince Charming, my rear end. Prince Prick is more like it.* He *is Molly Made.*

They were interrupted when trumpets heralded them to return to the ballroom. The lights dimmed, and once the crowd was assembled, a spotlight directed attention to the stage where the Fiddler Man, Caleb Weathers, was tuning up his fiddle. This gave Paige a chance to catch her breath and regain her bearing. Even as upset as she was, the scene unfolding in front of her was riveting. Caleb started fiddling *The Devil Went Down to Georgia,* and with the magic of computer-generated imagery, he played the rollicking tune alongside none other than the song's original fiddling artist, Charlie Daniels, holding the audience spellbound.

After the last fiddle note sounded, Caleb bowed to the crowds roaring applause as the lights came up.

Sunny tapped the mic again, clearly ready to announce the next event—as if that battle of the fiddles wasn't enough. "Ladies and Gents, didn't I promise you a night to remember? I'd say I delivered." She nodded to Caleb, thank you for an unforgettable experience. I need a drum roll, please."

The DJ complied, and Sunny exploded as she cried, "It's time for the big reveal. Unmask, everyone."

Folks obliged with playful digs, pokes, and punches accompanied by exclamations.

"I knew it,"

"You gotta be kiddin' me."

"How did you know it was me?"

Then Booker removed his mask, and Paige learned she was right. Booker was indeed her Prince Charming. *What a joke! A prince is supposed to be honorable and honest. A good catch worthy of a princess's love. Huh! Booker is a liar.* Granted, he didn't directly tell a lie, but he did withhold important information. He looked at Paige as she removed her glittering mask. The guilt of his betrayal reflected in his eyes as he shifted his weight, looking uncomfortable.

Sunny recaptured everyone's attention when she yelled, "Give it up, y'all, and put your hands together to welcome our surprise mystery guest, Miss Dolly Parton! She's here to sing us into tonight's closing event, the announcement of the Writers Triad Challenge winners. Let's give her a big ol' Southern welcome."

Dolly, in all her glittering, sparkling glory and stiletto heels, launched into her rendition of *We Are the Champions*, only she changed the pronouns throughout the song to *You*, and the audience went wild. The night definitely delivered all that Sunny promised.

Dolly finished her song and waved at the audience, pointing at individual people one by one. "Thank you. Y'all are the best, the champions of all time." She raised a silver fingerless gloved hand to her eyes to shield the glare and looked out at the assembly. "Will the Trinity Write authors please come up here? You have won the—now bear with me, y'all, this is quite a mouthful—the Aspiring Authors Collaboration Challenge Award." She swiped a hand across her brow. "Hurry now, get your tails over here. Y'all won!" Dolly paused, waiting for them to reach the podium on the dais.

Paige raised her hand to her mouth in disbelief, lifted her skirts, and began walking to the podium. She met up with Booker and Sunny on the ballroom floor. Sunny gaped at her, sagging a bit as Booker tried to help her through the throng.

Dolly continued laughing and clapping as they approached the podium. "Congratulations, writers, y'all won the Writers Triad Challenge. Your story, *Cape Cod Connections*, will be adapted for the Silver Screen. I'll be happy to write the score for it—as soon as I read it in the Great Smoky Mountain Anthology, that is." She handed each of them a trophy shaped like a silver feather-tip pen poised over the pages of an open book. The event and their names were etched on the pages.

Somehow, Paige smiled and made it through the accolades, speeches, and photos. She noticed that Booker avoided the cameras whenever he could and figured she now knew why. Even unmasked, his identity was still unknown to his faithful fans, who thought Molly Made was a woman. A large part of her wanted to spill the beans and tell the world who he actually was. *How did he get away with pretending to be a female writer for so long?* Millions of women believed Molly Made was a woman who understood their hearts, minds, and souls, not realizing that she was actually a he.

Her mind whirled through all the time they'd spent together writing and adventuring. Sure, he'd hinted here and there about people using a nom de plume—even admitted using one when they first met—but she hadn't put two and two together. Then the truth of it slammed into her. *He let me believe his lies. He tricked me and Sunny into believing he couldn't write as a woman. How could I be so stupid?*

She couldn't let herself get carried away, though. There were obligations and protocols in place to follow. Things expected of her, of them as the winning writers and collaborators. She'd have to pull an Academy Award performance and act like she was happy when she was not. No, she was upset, unsettled, so confused. Her head and heart were fighting a battle between truth and lies, love and loathing.

When it was Booker's turn to address the audience, he said, "Thank you for this honor. Let me tell you, I did not expect to win. I'm not sure any of us did. I'd like to thank you for this experience, and I hope you all enjoy our work as much as we enjoyed writing it." He stepped away from the mic and soon was surrounded by well-wishers, local television crews, and the press.

Paige turned away, but he grabbed her arm before she got far. "Wait. We need to talk."

She looked him in the eyes, seething with bitterness that filled her tone as she whispered in his ear, "There's nothing to say, *Molly*."

He visibly shrank, clearly shaken by her tone. "Please. Let me explain. It's not like it looks."

"Really," she deadpanned. "Your actions say it all. No photo ops, no book signings. I get it." Then she let the crowd carry him away, and in true Cinderella form, she fled. And yes, she lost a slipper, cast the other aside, and got the hell out of Dodge.

As soon as she could, she whipped out her phone and texted Alex.

Get me outta here. Now . . . airplane emoji . . . *Book me a ticket.*
Where to?
Paradise . . . palm tree emoji.
K

A few minutes later, he texted the information for a ticket to Hawaii.

She smiled and texted.

Meet me at the Hilton lobby on Airport Road.

Alex texted back with a thumbs-up emoji.

She sped down Airport Road and entered the Hilton Hotel. Apparently, no one cared that a barefoot Cinderella was waiting in the lobby. Either the hotel personnel had seen stranger things, or others had arrived in the ball gowns and costumes. Nobody gave her a second glance. *Who knows, who cares?*

Twenty minutes later, Alex showed up in the SUV instead of Craig Knight's monster truck. Tiny barked his hello from his crate, and she briefly acknowledged him with scratches through the bars.

Alex looked around. "Where's Prince Charming?"

"You mean Prince Prick? Somewhere in hell, I hope. Some prince he turned out to be." Then she burst into a flood of tears. Tiny whined in sympathy and pawed at his crate door.

"Care to talk about it?"

She choked out, "No."

Tiny started throwing a fit, so Alex pulled over as soon as he could and let Tiny out. Paige hugged her overgrown puppy and cried her eyes out into his fur.

Chapter Eighteen: Send in the Cav-alry

Time passed in a haze, and if asked, Paige would have a hard time remembering what she did, said, and saw after she ran from the ball. She simply took one step at a time, doing whatever came next as it arose. She didn't know if she'd told Alex to pack a bag for her or if he — being Alex — simply acted as efficiently as usual. All she cared about was that she no longer wore her Cinderella ballgown or bare feet but was dressed in leggings, boots, and a turtleneck with a lightweight duster to guard her against the cold. She would be leaving Tiny in Alex's care, so that was one thing she didn't have to worry about.

Alex looked strained on the drive to the airport, and he bombarded her with questions. "Shouldn't you sleep on this decision? Talk it out with someone? I'm here to listen. Are you acting too hastily? Are you sure you want to just up and leave? Do you realize there are still closing events you should be attending? There could be obligations associated with winning the WTC. You realize Sundance is involved, right? What about the screenwriting with Sunny and Booker... your writing trio?"

Paige remained silent, not answering any of Alex's questions. Her mind still floated in a haze, not wanting to think about anything except escape.

Alex pulled into the airport, which looked like a ghost town at such a late hour. Even the security checkpoint lines were empty. The next thing she knew, she was pulling up her ticket on her cell phone to remind herself where she was bound for. She looked at her screen, and her eyes popped when she read the destination—Hawaii. *Wowzer, leave it to Alex to pick the best paradise. Wonder if he packed the appropriate clothes.* She'd worry about her wardrobe when she got there.

She didn't know what she was going to do, and at this point, she didn't care. If she was a fool—and Booker's lies seemed to suggest she was—then she was a fool. Part of her felt like she'd been played, and that hurt . . . a lot.

Once settled into her first-class seat on the red-eye flight, she searched her purse for a sleep mask and tried to nurse her shredded heart. Her whole idea of finding Mr. Right was apparently nonsense. *Who says I need a man in my life? Okay, I did, but I didn't know what I was getting into. Yeah, I plotted it all out, but that plan didn't include betrayal. Happily ever after? Yes. I counted on that, but now . . . What was I thinking? I don't want a romance or a hero anymore.*

Her heart obviously felt differently. It felt completely over-shadowed by a very deep disappointment. Her broken heart told her she was in love and was paying a price she never dreamed she'd have to pay. *True, I set out to find my Mr. Right, and I thought I did. Who knew romance could be so messy?*

She paused a moment, lost in the imagery of a large feline paw clawing her bleeding heart into thin hanging strips. Blood droplets formed and dripped, each splat emphasizing her loss and pain. She raised her hand to her heart, trying to massage away the hurt. She curled into a ball of soul-searing anguish, folding into her cashmere duster. *I have only myself to blame. Yes, I succeeded in finding my guy. Too bad the consequences left me heartbroken and miserable. God, the pain.*

She tossed and turned. Tried one side, then the other, praying for respite and finally slipping into a light, restless sleep.

Flashbacks of Booker's thoughtfulness assailed her dreams

as he helped her in and out of vehicles or stepped aside so she could have the first view of the autumn mountain splendor. Pictures of him coaxing her across the suspension Skybridge, peering into the forested abyss below, brushing her hair from her eyes when they went up the Space Needle, finding a scrunchie he purchased from Ely's Mill for mountain walks when the winds blew. The smile he gave her at the Place of a Thousand Drips. Drinking hot cider together. How he looked bouncing with excitement when they went on the Big Orange Adventure tour. How protective he became when faced with an angry bear. The moonlit walks back to her cabin. How the firelight outlined his fit body.

The dream grew hotter as her mind replayed his tender touches. Her skin left sizzling by a flick of his tongue, followed by his warm mouth devouring her. She released a small moan and felt her back arch when she took the whole rock hardness of him inside her. She loved the feel and scent of him. Loved how comfortable he was in his skin. Loved how he wore his confidence like a wetsuit. Loved how he was at home no matter where he was.

When he touched her, it felt like she was in an out-of-body state of bliss, happy and excited, as he delighted her with his hot kisses. When he nibbled her neck, exquisite sensations and tingles zinged through her body. His mouth and kiss sent blood flooding her, making her core slick. He drank her as if her taste was intoxicating and her juices were an aphrodisiac. He intoxicated her the same way, and when his hands, fingers, and lips danced over her body, he became addicting. She craved his touch, his care, his concern, his body, and all that made him Booker.

A sudden chill made her shake. He was moving away from her, taking all his strength, warmth, and the feeling of safety with him, leaving her cold and more alone than ever. She had found something with Booker, but now he was gone, leaving her frozen, chilled to the bone, and afraid.

She wanted him back. Never had she felt so naked, lost, and bereft. She had lost what she'd set out to find. The blaze of his love was gone, and her confidence was shot. She had never noticed the absence of such deep desire before, but once that desire became satisfied, she knew she'd never be the same again. Not when he was gone.

She wanted him, and her dreams pointed out her loss, the enormity of feeling he left behind in the afterglow of just being in each other's arms, bed, life. Hot tears ran down her cheeks, and a sob escaped her lips.

Paige felt someone shaking her gently but insistently.

"Don't cry, honey chile, wake up. I'm Betina, and I'm here to help in any way I can." The voice belonged to a matronly flight attendant. "You must be dreaming. You're okay." The woman handed her a hot towel and sank into the empty seat next to her. "I don't know what's wrong. Was it a nightmare? Are you ill? Grieving? I can't do much since we're still an hour away from our destination. But I tell you what. When we land, and you see the sun rise over Hawaii, you'll perk up like a drooping Peace Lily plant after getting water. Sunrises always help whatever ails ya." The woman handed her a bottle of water. "Drink up. You could be dehydrated on top of it all."

Paige drank and shivered.

"Hm . . ." Betina surveyed her. "Some color is coming back to your face, but you're still trembling." She picked up Paige's cashmere duster, which had slid off Paige's shoulders, shook it out, then set it aside. In one stride, Betina was back with a plush sherpa blanket and draped it over Paige, tucking it in efficiently. As she bent to cover her, she said, "Lord Almighty. This airflow is on full blast. Cold air must have been blasting you all night. No wonder you're shaking like you're snow in a globe." She left for a minute, returning with another warmed towel and handing it to Paige. "Here ya go."

A splash of lemon scent bathed her senses as she used the warm cloth that seemed to magically restore her calm.

The kind vibes flowing from the woman were palpable. "I may be near retirement, but I got some life behind me, and I can tell you this. Things pass. Says so in the Bible. In the meantime, there's Tequila to help it along."

Paige laughed. "You say that like you know from experience."

Betina waved toward the other attendants. "Girl, with this crowd of *Genzers*, I hafta. I can do shots with the best of them. However, I don't recommend them before the sun rises." She shivered. "Heavens forbid."

Paige made a face. "Too bad."

"I can't serve you anything more now. In a few minutes, we'll start preparing for landing, but I promise you a sunrise over Hawaii will do wonders. Look outside." She pointed to the shuttered window beside Paige's seat. "May I?" At Paige's nod, she lifted the shade.

"It's still really dark out there," Paige remarked, her tone filled with doubt until she remembered the time difference. "It's still night here."

"Honey chile, it's always darkest before dawn."

And then the magic began. The deep darkness eased somewhat as she watched, turning the sky indigo instead of black. Then a lighter band appeared on the horizon, a shade of rose, followed by a hint of gold.

While Paige was used to rising at dawn, she never looked outside as the sun rose. By the time she fiddled with the vertical blinds in her writing room at home, the rising dawn had passed. Now she saw what she'd been missing and was amazed. The sky filled with golds, reds, bronzes, and oranges as the large ball of fire rose steadily, bathing the sky. Cumulus clouds seemed outlined with gold, and the sky popped with azure color as the sun burst free, rending the sky in blazing glory. It reminded her that a new day was indeed dawning, and it was gorgeous.

The cabin reverberated with the pong of the PA system, and the captain's mellow baritone welcomed them to the new day. "Aloha, folks. We're going to be in paradise in minutes. It's a balmy seventy-five degrees, no humidity, trade winds blowing five knots at Daniel K. Inouye International Airport in Honolulu. Welcome to Hawaii. Crew members, prepare for landing."

The few brave red-eyed passengers in first class stirred as they began to raise their seats, adjusting themselves, retrieving various items, and belting themselves for arrival. The kind, wise flight attendant melted away, straightening things and removing trash, helping prepare the craft and passengers for their landing.

Once Paige had straightened herself up, a different attendant, a bright-eyed young male carrying a silver-toned tray with rolled hot towels. Using tongs, he gave her another lemon-scented hot towel. If possible, it was even more refreshing than the one Betina had given her before. She looked out the window to see a string of emerald-green islands stretching out like beads of a necklace. As the plane seemed to hover over them and gradually descend, the islands began to show flashes of green, yellow, brown, and tan, like tiger-eye gemstones. Hawaii. Heavenly. Gorgeous. She should be thrilled, and she was, but it was tempered by loss.

Sunlight filled the cabin as they descended. Suddenly she felt three bumps, and they were speeding down the runway, the blue Pacific greeting them along with the towering palm trees. Even though she had been cold and shaken thirty minutes earlier, she felt transformed by the beauty outside and up for the challenge of rebuilding her broken heart.

Once they parked, Betina placed a lei of purple orchids around her neck and kissed her on each cheek, following ancient island culture. She winked. "Better days are coming, mark my words. Aloha."

CHAPTER NINETEEN: BLUE HAWAII

Paige didn't need to go to baggage claim, since all she had was a carry-on, and amazingly enough, her computer bag. Alex had thought of everything. While she could surely find a way to write if push came to shove, having her own laptop simplified things.

She spotted a man in an Aloha shirt holding a placard bearing her incognito pseudonym. Paige lowered her stylish sunglasses and said, "I'm Paige Smithfield."

"I'm Kikua Nihui, your driver. Since it's so early and there's little traffic, we'll get to the Princess K Hotel in no time. I'll take your things," he said, relieving her of her bags and walking her through the concourse. When they reached the ground transportation area, he led her to a white *Cadillac Escalade*, opened the passenger door, and offered a hand to help her if necessary.

As they left the airport, Paige gasped in surprise to see a full-fledged city with skyscrapers, not the lush green paradise she expected.

Kikua must have seen her expression and chuckled. "What? Bet you were expecting sand and sea and palm trees. Honolulu is a full-fledged city complete with a business hub, good restaurants, and active nightlife. Don't worry, though. You'll find the Hawaii people write home about soon enough."

Fortunately, the active city scene faded somewhat as the tall beachside hotels with their lavish and lush grounds unfurled like a fan.

Kikua pulled into the sweeping driveway of the Princess K Hotel. Porters rushed to receive them. He exchanged a few words and a laugh or two, then helped her exit the SUV. He transferred her bags to a porter sporting maroon slacks topped by a large plumeria print Aloha shirt, and another similarly dressed porter led the way to the Reception Terrace.

The open-roofed lobby took full advantage of island features, including palm trees and a to-die-for climate with gentle trade winds blowing through the reception area. Singing birds flew among the palm trees, becoming part of the hotel and creating a jungle-tropical ambiance. Carefully constructed sections for registering the guests flowed seamlessly amid stands of lava rocks. Only the distant pinging of the elevators reminded the tourists that they were in a hotel. Lush tropical plants and huge flower arrangements helped keep the real world of hotel operations out of sight. Comfortable wicker, teak, and rattan furnishings completed the look. The scene was delightful and wholly unexpected.

Paige felt the trade winds caressing her body and turned to see the nearby ocean sparking and catching the dazzling sunlight. The plethora of tropical flowers everywhere perfumed the air. A pert young islander, wearing a muumuu and a nameplate reading *Jasmine,* greeted her with a warm aloha and draped her neck with another lei — this one made of beautiful tiny shells.

While Paige had been to many great hotels, cities, and museums in Europe, she had little experience with the untamed natural beauty of places like the Smoky Mountains and Hawaii and no experience with tropical areas. Parts of her she hadn't known existed within her had opened while in the Smokies, but something here was bringing her more out of hibernation. This place had a pulse. She could feel it beneath the surface. While every plant, tree, and flower had been skillfully blended and tamed by the hotel's landscape artists, the wild and primitive essence of the island beat just underneath — moving, flowing, pulsing. The profusion and atmosphere of tropical splendor surrounding her became intoxicating.

A bellhop replaced the porter, and she followed him. They stepped into the elevator, and in no time, they reached the top floor. He held the doors open for her to pass, then quietly opened the double doors to her suite. He stepped aside so she could enter. Her breath stopped when she saw the aquamarine ocean stretching as far as the eye could see through the floor-to-ceiling windows. Graceful palms swayed in time with the trade winds near the shoreline in a dance as old as time. The young man gave her a few minutes to look her fill.

After a beat, the bellhop began cataloging the features of the suite. The décor was simple, reflecting the natural beauty of the island. The bathroom was sigh-worthy, boasting a heated toilet seat, a bidet, and a warm tush dryer. She vaguely heard the guy explaining room amenities, pool passes, and beach robes. The room's view drew her to the glass sliders that led to a wide balcony, and she stepped outside. An expanse of sea and surf lay before her and seemed to go on forever. She was certain only Eden could compete for awe-inspiring, and even then, it might lose.

She had never seen a view more enthralling, almost sensual, and engaging all her senses. She suddenly missed Booker like crazy as she stood before the sprawling ocean view, wishing he was sharing the completely bewitching sight.

Her sudden, intense yearning for Booker overcame her and knocked her off balance. She wanted Booker. Here. Right now. Taking her to the ultra-comfortable cushy bed that promised delights if only . . . No, she didn't want to surrender to the sweet dreams promise. She longed for the real feel of Booker's strong arms around her with her legs entwined around his thighs, enjoying his long, hard shaft inside her. She wanted him to engulf her, consume her with his passion, and experience the magic only he could deliver.

As the ocean waves rolled in leisurely outside, she yearned for Booker pounding deep inside her. She felt a rogue wave of overwhelming longing swamp her body. Her soul cried at the reality she faced. Booker. Was. Not. There.

The bellhop coughed discreetly, drawing her attention. With an effort, she brought her daydream under control as raw, unrequited need shattered around her like broken glass.

He bowed slightly when she turned to face him and asked, "Would you like a continental or full breakfast on the balcony?"

Until that moment, she hadn't given a thought to her basic needs. She wasn't tired, despite the restlessness of her sleep on the long flight, but she was hungry. "I'll have the full breakfast. Thank you."

After eating a wonderful breakfast with a garnish of vanda orchids perfectly placed on a plate of coconut pancakes, she sampled her first bite of the pineapple and learned what sunshine tasted like. It was imprisoned in the spikey plant's fruit. She licked her fingers, wiped them on her napkin, and started planning her day.

As she suspected, the outfits Alex had packed were way too warm for the tropical temperatures. She'd noticed several wonderful high-end stores on her way into the Princess K. Remembering her outline for finding a man and carefully orchestrating a change in her life, she frowned. *I'm just plain shopping this time, not for a man but for some knockout duds. Luxury Row, here I come!* She donned the lightest weight outfit she had and headed out the door.

The walk to Luxury Row didn't take long from the Princess K Hotel. The line of stores offered some of the finest brands in the world, including international retailers such as Chanel,

Gucci, Saint Laurent, Moncler, Bottega Veneta, and Miu Miu. She stopped in the Chanel and Gucci Stores and found several tops she adored that could easily pair with shorts, skorts, capris, or slacks. She picked up a rhinestone and denim bag.

Deciding she needed a sunhat, she tried on several and chose a sophisticated Audrey Hepburn style that would go with just about everything. She found a new zebra-patterned jumpsuit she just had to have, then tried on and bought a few lightweight sundresses, wrap dresses, and shorts. She added several pairs of sandals to her cache. All she needed then was a coverup and a bathing suit. After browsing through several with different kinds of asymmetrical features, she found a cute Polynesian suit with a tie at the hips. When she tried it on, she was happy to find it fit her as though it was made for her, like a tropical second skin.

She wore a short-wrap sundress and her transparent polymer wedge slider sandals out of the store and went in search of sunscreen, sundries, and a good romance. *I need a good novel.* She read the blurb on the back cover of the one she chose and thought romance novels should have warning labels. While she waited in line to pay, she texted Ned that she was off-grid . . . in Hawaii.

When Paige returned to the hotel, she lathered herself liberally with sunscreen, donned her new swimsuit, walked down to the cabana oceanside, and ordered a mai tai and Maui chips. After she nibbled and relaxed for a bit, she removed her new Gucci sunglasses, pulled her laptop out of her tote, and began to read her latest manuscript. The working title, *Southern Sirens*, was something she used to anchor her work and inspire her writing. She felt the tug to review the screenplay but resisted it . . . for now. The work of Trinity Write—aka Booker, Sunny, and herself—could wait.

Chapter Twenty: Home Sweet Home Tennessee

Sunny wasn't feeling her claim as Smoky Mountain's match-maker extraordinaire. She raised a hand to her forehead and tried to massage her emerging headache away. Her latest client, author Paige A. Newhart, famous for her plot twists, had pulled a plot twist herself.

Paige had taken off, fleeing the Fairy Tale Masquerade Ball just like her fictional counterpart Cinderella. Sunny had no idea where to start looking for her or what to do about the situation. But she was nothing if not resourceful. She left her toddler, Windy, with her twin sister Storme and hightailed it to the Sleeping Beauty cabin, hoping to find a clue to Paige's whereabouts. Their WTC team had unfinished business and a lot of work to complete. Not to mention the incomplete matchmaking side of things.

Once she reached the cabin, she let herself in, happy to see everything untouched since she had instructed the staff not to clean the cabin until further notice. She texted Alex.

Where's Cinderella?

AWOL

New York?

Nope.

Booker's?

I'll meet you at her cabin.

While Sunny waited, she looked for clues. Paige's posses-sions were strewn across the room. Her luggage was still sit-ting on the baggage rack. Tiny's toys were scattered here and there. That had to be a good sign.

She swept her gaze across the room, not noticing anything missing until it struck her. Paige's laptop was not there. *Oh. This is not good.* Sunny didn't see any remnants of her Cinderella costume, either. What had happened to that? And her *slippers*? She gulped. *Was Paige kidnapped?* She raised a hand over her pounding heart to still it. *What is the possibility of that? Like one in a hundred million? Do I notify Ranger Luke? His jurisdiction covers the premises . . . Do I call the police?*

Sunny was beside herself, feeling like a bee trapped in a mitten. Fortunately, Alex arrived. She ran to him, shaking his arm. "Where is Paige? Is she all right? Did someone abduct her? Does Booker know?"

"I can only tell you she's not here."

"No shit, Sherlock. I can see that."

Alex shifted his weight, clearly uncomfortable. He didn't meet her eyes. "She's not kidnapped—"

"Thank God! Where is she then?"

"MIA."

"Enough with the military talk," she ordered. "Again, I already know she's missing in action. Where *is* her ass?"

"I can't tell you that. I was ordered not to."

Sunny drilled down. *If he continues to go all military, so can I.* "Right here—in this cabin—I outrank her. I co-own this establishment. If my guest goes missing, I hafta bring in the big guns. You know what that means?"

"The police?"

"Worse. The *Press*. Social media will be on this like geese on June bugs!"

Alex gulped and cleared his throat. "I can't disclose that information, but I'll give you some clues. Listen carefully for them."

Sunny put her hands on her hips while her right foot drummed the floorboards. "You better talk to me, bud."

"I can't tell you much, but maybe she got ahold of her

editor. Ned might know what she's doing. I think that's part of her contract."

"Give me his phone number pronto," Sunny commanded. "His *private* line."

Alex scrambled to retrieve Ned's contact data. "I'll text it. But we need to come up with a plan. She's upset with Booker, and she booked outta here. Took the first plane out, a red eye. There's an ocean involved, a time change, but no passport needed." He gave more hints. She's reachable but . . ."

"So she's in the USA?"

He nodded. "Kinda."

"Is it tropical?"

Again, he nodded.

"The Virgin Islands?"

He shook his head. "Wrong ocean."

A light went on. *Transcontinental. Hmm. Transpacific? Hawaii! Booker! I knew there was trouble in paradise. Must be a lovers' spat.* Sunny's wheels were already turning. She snapped her fingers. *Got it.* All she had to do was a little finaglin'. She was born for such moments as this. She pulled all her marketing experience, writing skills, and matchmaking abilities together and hatched her plan.

"Get Ed, Ted—"

"Ned."

"Whatever. Get him on the line and get him talking. Find out if he can get Paige to do a little favor for him or issue an order, or something. I gotta get to my computer."

Alex saluted. "Aye, aye, Captain."

"Enough with the military references."

She returned to her cabin and began a Google search. *Perfect. This will work.* She called the number she'd found with a Hawaiian exchange.

The call connected with a recorded message. "Solo No Mo, Pair-A-Sailing. Find your match today. Sail with us to find your mate. To speak to a representative, press or say *one.* For pricing and group rates, press or say *two*. For a reservation, press or say *three*. How may I direct your call?"

"Three." And just to be sure, she added, "Reservations."

Within minutes, after a little dose of Sunny magic, she managed to book two reservations for parasailing appointments. It was time to launch *Operation Booker*. She drummed her fingers on her desk. *Hmm, now to figure out how to get Booker to Hawaii . . .*

Her phone pinged with a text from Alex with Ned's contact info. Alex added that she should be the one to convince Ned to do whatever she wanted. She chuckled, and seconds later, she got Ned on the line. After some fast talking, she enlisted his cooperation and blessing. Turned out Ned was concerned, too.

She then turned her attention to the templates on her computer. She created her matchmaker masterpiece and sent it off to Ned, who would pull a few strings with colleagues and get it to Booker. Mission nearly accomplished. All she had left on her list was to get Booker ready, willing, and on his way to sail into the sunset. *Good grief. Now I'm all nautical.*

"Ahhh," Sunny sank back into her seat, feeling accomplished. She'd done it . Operation Booker was a *go*. Ned would make sure the WTC winners received their invitations and reservation info for a Hawaii celebration. She smiled. *Chemistry will do the rest, I'm sure.*

Chapter Twenty-One: Surprise

Paige couldn't put her triad work aside any longer. She decided to review their story before it got published in the anthology and to prepare for writing the screenplay. Normally, before even opening a WIP, she'd consult her detailed outline and make notes using color codes and larger fonts so she could easily identify the chapter in a later work session. Yet she wasn't doing that this time. Quite the opposite. She just started reading.

Typically, she'd make decisions to alter, delete, or keep as she read. She wasn't doing that either. *Maybe it's because I'm distracted by Booker. Or have jet lag. Or it could be because I never wrote a screenplay before and am not clear on how to start.* She wasn't sure, and that bothered her.

She usually had no problem retreating into her work and getting through whatever else she might have to face, but not this time. She knew writing a screenplay would be very different and quite challenging. She wondered if she should even attempt it without her collaborators. For all she knew, Booker or Sunny might have some experience somewhere in their career.

She closed her eyes and relaxed for a moment, enjoying the sunshine, the ambiance, and the tropical breeze. She decided to just read through the story — period — no changes or notes. She let out a deep sigh and tried to get control of her urge to edit. *Just read it, damn it.*

As she read, she quickly noticed similarities that mirrored a lot of what she and Booker faced. The Nathaniel and

Patience characters were opposites with different tastes in foods, work styles, and preferences in general. Yet their attraction and feelings for each other came across strongly. Each character cared about the other's well-being. Their character arcs were clear as the story progressed. Both found that making some minor alterations in their lifestyles could complement the other. *How did I not see this before? Did Sunny manipulate the story plot while maneuvering me and Booker in her matchmaking scheme?*

It didn't take a genius to see herself as Patience and Booker as Nathaniel. The similarities were staring her in the face, clear as a bell. What happened in the story was occurring between Booker and Paige.

She finished reading and quickly exited the document, but her thoughts weren't as easily dismissed. She couldn't help but wonder if she and Booker would experience the same happy ending. *Didn't Sunny giggle and hint several times about not seeing the forest for the trees? It appears she was right about that.*

She took stock, surprised to note that she, like Patience, had made several changes in her life during the conference. She was rising later, for one thing, and wasn't writing from six a.m. to six p.m. She'd altered her schedule to accommodate Sunny's childcare arrangements and Booker's chronology. She was trying different foods, too. She had even eaten corndogs and funnel cakes with Booker.

Paige had nothing against picnics, but five-star dining was more her style. Yet she'd picnicked several times with Booker and Sunny and enjoyed it. In the past, she never let herself eat junk food, but Booker was addicted to cheese puffs, and now so was she. Obviously, her life had changed since she'd met Booker. A pang of loss pierced her heart.

She had never been adventurous before, either, but she had gone to the top of the Arcadia Space Needle despite her fear of heights. Throughout the convention, she'd often joined outdoor workshops and work sessions, spending more time outside and loving it. She'd previously ignored the natural beauty that this conference — and Booker — introduced her to. He'd even convinced her to try the Alpine Slide at Ober Mountain after they crossed the Skywalk Suspension Bridge at Sky Park.

For the first time, she questioned her new impetuous actions. She gasped, realizing her life over the past weeks had been more spontaneous than flying to Hawaii. *This is not like me. What's happening? Have my hormones gone to my brain and short-circuited me?*

To regain her footing, she tried doing something *typical Paige* style. She pulled up her *Find Mr. Right* outline to try and recapture what she wanted and how she planned to get there. She paused and took a quick look at her outline.

Opening the document again, she amazed herself, bemused by what she'd meticulously planned. But it was all there in black and white.

She mentally checked off the points, noticing she hadn't done most of what was listed. *No speed dating.* The same was true of attending church to meet someone. *When was the last time I even graced the inside of a church? Grocery shopping? Who am I kidding? I don't grocery shop. Elyse does it online and has it delivered.* A small voice inside her head reminded her that she was looking to find a man, a potential date, a mate. Racing — running — away to Hawaii was not included in her list.

She read on and found she hadn't had a meeting by chance take place, much less a cute meet-up. Then, like a bolt of lightning, it hit her. She'd met Booker in a cute, chance meeting and hadn't even realized it. She placed another checkmark on her list. It looked like Booker accounted for most of the ticked-off items.

Next up were the dependency issues. Those would take some additional thought. While marriage meant intimacy, the nature of the beast bred some codependence. However, with

Booker, she was learning flexibility, accommodation, and compromise, which earned her another check-off.

Another checkpoint on the list was common interest, which was a no-brainer. With all their time together, Paige had discovered she and Booker had quite a bit in common. Both were successful and loved writing, even though their creative processes were different. The Big Orange Jeep Tour proved many of their likes and interests were similar, and their compatibility was beyond question in and out of bed.

She felt herself blush, remembering how it felt to feel his skin on hers and the arousal she experienced when they kissed and cuddled. He was so comfortable in his own skin, exuding a confidence that was a big plus for her. It made her feel safe and secure in his arms.

There were some things on the list she wasn't quite ready for just yet. The house, a spouse, and children were considerations for later. Yes, she wanted love, marriage, and the baby carriage, but now was not the time.

As she reviewed the checkmarks on her outline, it hit her like an avalanche. She had already found her hero and fallen in love. With Booker . . . Now, she had some thinking to do.

A server appeared dressed in the same plumeria Aloha shirt that the porters and bellboys wore—*must be a signature look for the hotel staff*—paired with long maroon board shorts and a Koa nut lei around his neck. He held a small bamboo tray toward her, lowering it so she could reach the tropical drink concoction. "Enjoy your Blue Hawaiian, miss."

The drink, served in a carved-out pineapple, was decorated with a spear of coconut, a vanda orchid, a plastic palm tree drink stirrer, and a paper umbrella.

She sipped it through a straw. *Mm, delicious.* "Thank you, but where did this come from?"

The waiter smiled and quipped, "From the poolside bar."

Smart aleck. "How do you say *ha, ha, ha* in Hawaiian?"

He chuckled and said, *"Mo ho'omāke'aka."*

"Huh?"

"That's how you say *ha, ha, ha* in Hawaiian."

She threw him a wicked look. "Seriously, *who* sent this?"

He gave her a wide grin and a wink, and then pointed to the envelopes on the tray with a flair.

She opened the heavy stock missive and read . . .

Aloha, Paige. Enjoy the drink and your unexpected stay. To keep your brand going, open the next envelope and have some fun while you're there. Remember, the planned photo ops we'll get are very important. Ned.

Paige grumbled. "How do you say *smart aleck* in Hawaiian?"

The server winked again. "Akamai aleck."

"You said it, not me."

She turned her attention to the larger envelope, emblazoned with a company name, *Solo No Mo.* It contained a lanyard sporting a laminated name tag — with her name — and a card that read, *Look for your match. Number three, three, three.* She looked at the date and time. *Holy Shit.* It was dated the next day at sunset for a duo parasail. The attached brochure read, *Find your mate while Pair-A-Sailing. Look for the number three, three, three to find your date.*

Paige was thunderstruck. Parasailing was *not* on her bucket list. Then she remembered her outline. It implied trying new things, and *Solo No Mo* fit the bill.

She chuckled. She had to admit it was clever marketing. Plus, she'd find a way to chalk it up to her brand and provide another check mark on her list. *Not too shabby.*

Deciding she had enough sun for the day, she packed up and returned to her room. She texted Sunny, letting her know she'd be working remotely and suggesting a *Zoom* meeting for the next day. She'd have to figure out the time difference to work around Sunny's childcare schedule and Booker's . . .

She ordered room service and enjoyed her mahi mahi dinner on her ocean-facing balcony while watching the aquamarine waves curl lazily onto the golden sands of Waikiki. Hawaiian music drifted from a nearby restaurant, adding a dreamy tropical touch. Too bad she was busy mourning the demise of her relationship with Booker. *I feel like a fool. So stupid. He was upfront — to a degree. He joked that he'd have to kill me if he fessed up to his true identity. Why didn't I challenge that?* But she knew why. She hadn't planned on falling in love with him. *I knew he had a nom de plume, but I never expected him to be Molly Made. My nemesis.* There was no denying it after watching him sign that contract — she had seen the signature a million times before.

He had led her to believe he wrote action thrillers. *Yet did he? Or did I jump to the conclusion because of his rugged looks? Regardless, I still feel betrayed that he didn't trust me with the truth.* He'd flat-out deceived her by withholding important information about himself. Of that, there was no doubt.

Still, she missed his wit. His charm. His skill in bed. The fun they had together. A million images of him filled her mind, playing like a movie on the silver screen in full technicolor. She pictured his smile when he saw her each day. His fine frame — broad shoulders, narrow waist tapering to a tight man butt — assaulted her mind's eye. And talk about his natural scent. A woodsy blend of cedar and pine, fresh and arresting. And his kiss. Wild but gentle, firm but not unpleasant.

Thinking of Booker got her girly parts throbbing and wishing he were there to release them. The tropical setting certainly awakened her senses in a way very different from the colorful beauty of the Smokies. She stared out at the vibrant green landscape as she remembered Booker's kisses and touches.

Restlessness had her getting up from her finished meal and ordering a tropical nightcap to go with her first Hawaiian sunset. *Only one thing missing . . . Booker.*

Once the sun set, the sudden darkness seemed dramatic. It took a while for her sight to adjust to the dim lighting of the hotel that begged lovers to seek the nearest bed.

Jet-lagged and mildly hung-over — one Mai Tai and Blue Hawaii too many — Paige began her day with a shower. The body wash provided by the hotel felt delightful. She lathered her sun-assaulted skin carefully upon finding she'd got more sun than she thought.

She dressed casually in shorts, a sunhat, and a cropped top after slathering a generous dollop of aloe-laced sunscreen. She grabbed her bag and went down the elevator to the oceanside restaurant, looking forward to a pineapple pancake feast — minus the Mimosa — served with a piping hot cup of Kona coffee and people-watching.

Judging by the screams of delight and laughter from tourists in stylish swimwear, they were already surfing, swimming, and having a blast. She planned to join them soon. The server arrived with her plate of artfully arranged pancakes and her coffee, placing them before her.

She took a bite and swooned. "I don't think anything can beat these."

He winked. "Wait until you taste the brew."

She raised the mug to her lips and sipped. "Heavenly."

He smiled and left her.

The view and the food were entertaining enough. She didn't want to ruin it by calling up her email or the document, but duty tugged at her. *They're all probably sleeping anyhow.* But when she checked the time, she was shocked to see how late it was back in the Smokies. Alarm raced through her until she remembered the five-hour time difference between Hawaii and Gatlinburg. Maybe it wasn't too early to check in with them. *To hell with it. I'm my own person. I don't need to check in with anyone.*

She wanted to try new things and had succeeded so far. She had, after all, just slept in. She was still a free agent. At least until her evening sail with Solo No Mo.

She charged her breakfast to her room and went upstairs to change into her cute new sarong-style swimsuit. She slathered on more sunscreen, donned her cover-up, and headed for the beachside cabana carrying her phone. Once settled in her lounge chair, she took one look at the languid Pacific and released a long sigh of pleasure. She'd be in heaven if only Booker . . .

With determination, she cast him from her thoughts. Tried to, at least.

She spent the afternoon lounging on the beach, glad she had the advantage of the cabana's sun protection. Before ending her lazy day—another first for her—she decided to answer the call of the glorious ocean, learning firsthand what all the squeals and laughter were all about. The sea wrapped her in its salt-water arms, and she enjoyed the feel of every wave lifting and setting her down. Then an unexpected wave knocked her under the surface, but she came up from the water, sputtering and laughing. Her baptism in the Pacific invigorated her spirit.

Once she'd dried off, she returned to her suite, showered, and changed into cute capris and a midriff top, adding a pair of sensible sandals she hoped were appropriate for her next adventure. Armed with her lanyard and invitation, she stopped by the concierge's desk and ordered a cab to take her to Solo No Mo.

After a short ride, the cab driver pulled into the dock's drop-off plaza. She enjoyed the steady but balmy trade winds skimming across her skin as the cab driver directed toward a guy bearing a sign reading *Solo No Mo*. She headed that way, joining a small group of anxious but eager people gathered around him.

When the crowd settled and stared at the man with the sign, he set the sign aside and all but shouted. "You malihinis, newcomers to the island, have a one-hour ticket for a sunset Pair-a-sail, so you'll be solo no mo." He winked. "Cute name, no?"

The couples in the group laughed.

"I am your host Temu Ranu. That means I tell you what to do. You do. Or you *make*." He ran a finger across his throat to translate his meaning.

Silence fell over the crowd.

"Ha ha, just kidding."

The group chittered, some giggled, most looked relieved.

"Let's rock and roll." Temu waved his arms and bent his knees, looking up at them wryly. "When you hear the word *aloha*, you s'pose to say the same in return. Otherwise, you don't sound like you in the islands, you know? Repeat after me. Aloha!"

"Aloha." Only Paige and some of the crowd muttered the greeting.

He gestured madly. "Come on now. You can do betta."

"Aloha." More of the group joined in with a bit more vigor.

"What's that?" Temu held a hand to his ear. "That weak excuse for a welcome doesn't cut it. Let's try again. Aloha!" he shouted louder this time.

Paige let out an enthusiastic bellow along with everyone else. "Aloha!"

"I knew you could do it. Here in Hawaii, we give you aloha, love. You give it back. That's the aloha way. Now, step this way."

He then headed toward another group Paige hadn't noticed before. He walked like an Egyptian in an old MTV video, so she and the others got into the spirit of things, relaxing and laughing, and walked like an Egyptian, too. When he swayed into a hula, everyone followed his lead.

"You ready to rumble?" Temu asked. "Or shall we say sail away?"

Thunderous cheers erupted.

"Oh, I see. So now you wanna be solo no mo, huh?"

Another cheer went up.

He held up his arms, gesturing for silence. "Okay. Now you are ready. These Hawaiian lovelies will greet you in the manner of our people."

Two young men and two young gals approached, draping shell lies around the attendees' necks and kissing them once on each cheek.

"Now it's time to check your lanyards, wahines, ladies — or women if you prefer — and kanes, gents," Temu called out. "Each of you was given a code to lead you to your match. Don't hesitate, or you'll miss your date."

People shuffled about, examining their piece of laminated plastic, and set off to find their mate. Heads down, peering at their codes, several people bumped into others and laughed their way to their match. Paige went in search of hers, too. She noticed the PR team was ready to catch the moment and took it in stride.

She looked down, double checking her code, when she saw a pair of well-corded, trim male legs. *Hm. Nice man-gams.* She looked again. And again. They looked oddly familiar.

She looked up to chest level and saw the lanyard with a three, three, three code. A match. She lifted her gaze to face level. "You!"

"You?"

"What the hell is this?" The ice in her tone was designed to indicate he'd need more than a sweater to warm up, he'd need a zero-degree thermal parka.

CHAPTER TWENTY-TWO: SHOCK WAVE

Paige looked around to try to find some kind of metaphorical hook to hang her nerves on. *Booker Turner!* Her shock bled sound from the world. Her ears heard nothing. She wanted to take flight, but someone eased her into a lifejacket and a harness all in one slow motion. "What are you doing here?"

"What are *you* doing here?" Booker asked at the same time.

"Pair-a-sailing," they echoed as one.

"We have to stop meeting like this, Paige." His tone held a hint of sarcasm and something else she could not name.

Longing? Joy? Wistfulness?

"This is ridiculous," she said as they fiddled with his lifejacket and harness.

"Agreed."

Paige glared at him. "This must be one of Sunny's matchmaking schemes."

They were interrupted when Temu started giving instructions, explanations, and directions, including something about promising a surprise ending, a real splash. It all sounded like the *wah wah wah* of Charlie Brown's teacher. In a haze, she let them lead her onto the launch boat. The next thing she knew, she and Booker were attached to the parasailing rig — in tandem. *Some pair we make.*

Once they lifted off, according to Temu's information, their feet and legs dangled eight hundred feet off the ground. Below lay the blue Pacific like a carpet.

While hovering above the water, Booker said, "We have

unfinished business to discuss."

She gave a mirthless laugh. "To say the least."

"Smile."

She gaped at him. "What?"

"For the cameras. See?" He pointed to the PR people and the mounted camera catching everything.

Paige recalled Temu saying they were sailing in Maunalua Bay. As they sailed, serenity warred with the June bugs competing with the butterflies in her stomach. Even the stunning beauty of Diamond Head resting beside the sea and its splendor couldn't distract her from the sheer masculinity of the man hanging next to her. His warmth seeped into her body, so starved for his touch, his kiss, his dick. She wanted to strangle and thrash him as much as she needed to make love to him and never stop.

He reached for her hand. "We need to talk."

"So you said. About what, *Molly Made*?"

He winced. "About that."

"You lied to me. How could you?"

"I tried hard not to."

"Oh yeah, I nearly forgot about your *If I tell you, I'll have to kill you* speech. That's still deception. I repeat, how could you?"

He frowned. "You won't like the truth."

"Try me."

The trade winds bounced them a bit, and she refocused on the beautiful view. "This is amazing." She sighed, then turned to face him again. "What's your excuse?"

"There is no excuse."

"Really? You led me to believe you were a debut author—"

"You heard what you wanted to hear. I did not imply that, but in my defense, there is an explanation."

"Hmph. Oh?"

"I write as Molly Made—"

"My nemesis. You let me throw shade—"

"I couldn't explain or defend against that. Keeping my identity secret increases sales, earns likes on social media, promotes my brand, and counters the premise that men can't write convincing romances and get taken seriously by the female market. There are some contractual issues . . ."

"So, it boils down to the almighty dollar."

He sounded frustrated, his voice clipped. "Yes. You could say that."

She glared at him. "But you chose not to tell *me*. After everything we've been through . . . What else will you keep from me?"

"I'll tell you whatever you want to know, but I have a solid and serious reason for holding back full disclosure about Molly. I'm a nobody, but Molly Made is a brand."

"Oh?"

"I signed a hefty nondisclosure clause. Telling anyone breaks my contract. Molly Made is fiction, but a lot of other jobs depend on her. I'm real. What you see is who I am. I'm Maximilian Mollins Booker Turner. I'm the guy who's afraid of needles, loves my rescue dog, and cries when couples marry or when dogs die, hell I cry at the movies. I'm still the guy who is into nature and loves football and lazing in a jacuzzi with a certain sexy woman. Those are not lies. It's who I am. None of that has changed. And I'm still the guy who loves you."

She turned away and said, "And I'm the gal you deceived. I don't know if I can trust you anymore."

Booker sighed. "There is that. I suppose there's not much more I can say or do to change your mind."

A glorious spectacle of brilliant color spread across the sky, making it officially the best sunset ever and the saddest night of her life. The Pair-A-Sail captain chose that moment to dip them into the sea, ending their flight and conversation with the splash he had promised earlier.

Chapter Twenty-Three: Sail Away

Paige and Booker were silent on the way back to the dock. Booker's face was set, as though he was resigned to the fate she had set for them.

When they disembarked, Booker walked her to the parking plaza. "I'm sorry," he said as he hugged her, his arms feeling like home.

"I am, too." She sighed. "The damage is done."

"Looks like it. Have a good trip home. I'll be in touch. To write the screenplay."

She nodded, wanting to fold into his parting hug. She felt broken. Emotions careened around her like fishflies milling around a streetlight.

She texted for a taxi and headed back to her hotel. During the drive, she was struck by the lit tiki torches lining the beach, highlighting lovers strolling hand in hand in the moonlight, making it the perfect ending to a night after that blazing sunset. The scent of tropical flowers perfumed the air that breezed through her open window. How she wanted to be with her lover, too. Tears filled her eyes, threatening to spill down her cheeks. *Booker and I should be sailing away into the sunset.*

Paige tipped the cab driver, entered the hotel feeling like a bizarro version of Cinderella, and headed for the tiki torch-lit patio. She ordered a Mai Tai as the musicians in muumuus and grass skirts played Ahola 'Oe.

She tried hard not to think of Booker's scent, his touch, his strong arms around her, or the way he made love with her.

Tried but failed miserably. Despite all the lies, half-truths, and disinformation, she still wanted him desperately. But she was not desperate enough to renege on her decision, much less forgive him. It would only end in a lifetime of lies.

If only thoughts of him didn't constantly fill her brain.

Her mind replayed how sexy he appeared in the morning, how handsome he looked as Prince Charming, how strong he felt when helping her board the Big Orange jeep, his thoughtfulness when he draped a towel around her after using the Spa Haus, the kindness he showed when letting a fussy baby and harassed mother go ahead of them in line at the ticket kiosk, his mischievous smile when he handed her a mason jar of hot cider laced with moonshine, his sweet kisses, how wet he made her. She finished her drink and fled like Cinderella at the stroke of midnight, heading back to her room with a perfect view of the stars, moonbeams, and gentle midnight surf.

Paige tried to shut down her wayward thoughts. When that failed, she took a hot bubble bath, soaking until the water cooled. She tried to forget the feel of Booker caressing her body, playing with her clit, or his hardness probing her gently. She'd experienced the ecstasy he brewed within her, and now she learned the agony of being without him.

She slipped into her silk nightdress, picked up her laptop, opened their story, and started reading, concentrating on adapting it to a screenplay. As she read, she once again noticed Sunny's skillful matchmaker manipulation of the story. What she read mirrored her and Booker's story with different names, times, and settings. It was all there in black and white. Their love story.

All the key elements were there as clear as a sunny day. The plot had a few twists she hadn't noticed before, but she saw Booker's input in a new light. *Patience the heroine was writing as a man and didn't tell Nathanial her nom deplume. How different when the shoe was on the other foot.* Paige was shocked when the hero didn't condemn the heroine for doing what Booker did in real life. Not at all. No, Nathaniel *applauded* Patience's ingenuity.

While Paige condemned Booker for nondisclosure and sentenced their relationship to the death penalty, Nathanial praised, understood, and granted Patience grace.

Paige had made herself judge and the jury, pronouncing Booker guilty without granting due process, without his *innocent until proven guilty* legal right. No, Paige had shown no mercy, no clemency, no understanding. Instead, she'd pronounced death by lethal injection, knowing full well from firsthand experience that Booker hated needles. She hadn't given him a chance, much less a trial. *Even criminals get a second chance.*

She hung her head. She wanted to run to him, make up for her rush to judgment. She wanted a second chance. Would Booker be like Nathanial and give her another chance?

Booker took a rideshare to his private plane parked at the Honolulu International Airport. If he hadn't owned a jet, had it not been at his disposal, he could never have made the transit in time to be with Paige. He stomped up the stairs. *What the hell happened to innocent until proven guilty? What part of the breach of contract and nondisclosure doesn't Paige understand? As a writer, she knows that you need some anonymity to write the next page-turner and get it into the fans' hands. I didn't choose to deceive her. I couldn't – legally – reveal my identity to her or anyone. She knows that.*

Booker opened the document and began to write his notes for the screenplay and got the shock of his life. He read on and then scrubbed his face and chuckled. The story they had written was the romance he was having with Paige. He couldn't wait to see how she'd react when they met up again for the closing event. He smiled ear to ear.

CHAPTER TWENTY-FOUR: INTO THE SUNSET

Paige woke up the next morning and tried to find Booker. Due to hotel privacy regulations and policies, no one would confirm his occupancy. Short of hiking off to hunt him down, she tried to call him, but it went straight to voicemail. *I don't want to leave a message for this. I'll fly home and try him face to face. The writer's retreat ends soon, but I have time to get back before the closing ceremony. Closing remarks are set for the Ogle Terrace in two days.* She booked an overnight flight back to the mainland. It'd be close, but she had the time to pull it off.

Then she received a text from Sunny.

Screenwriting Zoom *meeting is set up for thirty minutes from now.*

Paige ignored it and did not participate. She did watch through their shared document app, though.

About ninety minutes later, her phone pinged. She saw Sunny was calling her on FaceTime.

Paige sighed and answered the call. Sunny's face wasn't happy and supportive. No, she appeared madder than two hens fighting over a worm.

Sunny drummed her fingers on the desk in front of her. "What's going on? This is a big deal you're blowing off. A career-maker for me, and it won't hurt you or Booker either. What gives?"

Paige hung her head. She felt her face freeze. "I just couldn't face him then. Now I've boxed myself into a corner."

"I presume you read our work."

"Of course I have. I sent my comments and got the attachments from you and Booker." They talked for a few minutes, bringing Paige up to speed. She shared bits of her dilemma with Booker.

Then Sunny scrunched her eyes, giving Paige the *look*. "Okay. Now tell me. What would one of your strong female characters do in your shoes?"

Paige went silent as images filled her brain and danced through her head.

"Paige, answer me. Would Patience bail in a similar situation? Would she slink off into the night? Let her love slip away?"

Inspiration struck Paige.

"Yoohoo. Earth to Paige. Paige? Answer me."

Paige looked up. "Sorry about that. I was plotting." An idea took shape. "No. Patience would drop everything and take care of business. She wouldn't eat crow, though."

"No one asked you to. We simply want to get this thing written."

"You're a genius, Sunny, thanks. Gotta go!"

Paige texted Alex to pick her up at the airport, giving him her flight info and arrival time. She was going back. A little while later, Alex texted that he and Tiny couldn't wait to see her. She packed and got herself ready for the flight back.

Paige made it to the airport in plenty of time. As she exited the cab, she was greeted by a gentle trade wind filled with the scent of gardenias, wishing her a sweet goodbye. She settled in the airport lounge until the call to board her flight interrupted her thoughts.

Sunny had mentioned a mystery speaker was set to close the conference. Paige had caught Sunny's subtle hints that it might be someone she knew. She had an idea of who it would be. Whether it was or wasn't didn't affect her plan much.

She walked to the gate, showed her ticket on her cell phone, and boarded. She was tired but optimistic. She pulled out her noise-blocking headset and sleep mask, put her cell on airplane mode, and reclined her first-class seat. She intended to sleep her way home since she hadn't slept well the night before. Once they were in the air, the steady hum of the aircraft lulled her to sleep in no time.

Eight hours later, a gentle shake woke her up.

"We'll be landing soon." The flight attendant handed her a heated towel to help her ease into the day. The time change made it late afternoon. It'd be a short drive from the airport outside of Knoxville to Pigeon Forge. *Amazing what some sleep, dream sex with Booker, and time do for clarity. I need Alex . . .*

She texted Alex.

ETA in thirty minutes. C U soon. Get a helicopter ready.

He texted back.

?

Rent. A. Helicopter . . . asap.

He responded with a thumbs-up emoji.

After meeting and catching up with Alex and watching his histrionics when she told him what she intended, she finally persuaded him to take her to the helipad in Pigeon Forge. Once there, she told them she'd need a parachute and explained her plan. It cost her a bundle, but that was what money was for. After some intense instruction, she was set to go.

In mere minutes, she was hovering over the Gatlinburg Convention Center Ogle Terrace. They ran through what they would do, what Paige would do, and how. *I'm doing this. I'm jumping right into my plan.* Once again, Paige donned a harness and parachute, but her flight wouldn't be over an ocean this time. No, she'd be para sailing into the Smoky Mountains.

She got into position once she was rigged up. They slid the

copter door open. The wind rushed in, blowing her hair around her goggles. The crewman signaled. It was Go time. *It doesn't matter if this idea is bonkers or if Alex thinks I'm crazy. It's too late now.* She jumped.

She created quite a stir when she landed — surprisingly — exactly where she intended. Sunny and several attendees rushed over to help her out of her parachute and harness. She quickly thanked them and hurried to the mic, where Booker stared with a shocked open-mouth expression.

"Excuse me for dropping in unexpectedly like this and interrupting what I'm sure was a fascinating closing speech. Something about honesty and surprises, I'd bet. But I have a plot twist. I promise it will be a page-turner and a worthy read." She got down on one knee. "Booker Turner, will you marry me?

"Hell yes, Paige Newhart!" Booker said. "But what about our issues?"

"We worked out the differences between Nathanial and Patience in our story. I'm confident we can write a happily-ever-after for us as well." She leaned in and whispered in his ear, "I get it. For your brand, anonymity is critical."

He gave her a whopping movie kiss, bending her backward. When she straightened, she kissed him back with everything she had. Booker lifted her into his arms just like the silver screen heroines of the nineteen-fifties.

Her PR people — filming it all for the Paige Newhart brand — went nuclear.

When things settled down, and the last of the hoots, hollers, claps, and clamor stopped, he said, "Our marriage will make you Paige Turner."

She laughed and winked. "With a storybook ending."

He threw his head back and laughed. "And a made-for-TV ending as well."

Paige took his hand and headed for the sunset amid a new

burst of thunderous applause. The PR folks snapped and filmed every spectacular second.

Sunny greeted them as they left the terrace, dusting her hands, and deadpanned, "My work here is done. Cinderella found her fella. After all, I did promise y'all a surprise ending. Did I not?" She blew on her fist and buffed her nails on her chest. "Am I a good matchmaker or what? I predict Booker and Paige Turner will live happily ever after."

The End

OTHER BOOKS BY KATHY KALMAR

The Beach Series

Beyond the Beach Book One
Beyond the Beach Book Two
Beyond the Beach Book Three
Beyond the Beach Book Four
Beyond the Beach Book Five
Back to the Beach Book One
Back to the Beach Book Two
Promises on the Beach

The Mountain Series

Mountain Hot
Mountain Christmas
Mountain Skye Prequel to the Weather Girls
Mountain Kiss
Mountain Joy
Mountain Promises
Mountain Holly
Mountain Silver
Mountain Mistletoe
Mountain Bred
Mountain Led
Mountain Wed
Mountain Hookup
Mountain Fever

ABOUT THE AUTHOR

Kathy Kalmar, born in Detroit, Michigan, lives with Larry, her husband of four-plus decades. Lately, her life has recovered from the bad country song-like life because her Smoky Mountain Tops Round House is rebuilt from the 2016 Chimney Tops II Wildfire, and she is writing her next book in her Writing Room. Her current residence is enlarged by four feet with the addition of their new puppy. She loves to read and write contemporary romance novels. Meanwhile, she remains fond of hot tubbing, chocolate, sipping wine, mai tais, and moonshine at home, Waikiki, Tennessee, and Cape Cod. Y'all come back, hear?

Contact Kathy at KathyKalmar.com

www.ingramcontent.com/pod-product-compliance
Lightning Source LLC
Chambersburg PA
CBHW071235130626
46556CB00003B/1017